Year of the Horse

'One specific year stands taller; it came like no other.'

Shejee Hunter

Book Cover by

Christine Laurenson

Year of the Horse

In loving memory of my dear friends

Doreen and Derek James Wood

«Prologue»

'The fabric of life is not complete without the thread of time. The measure of time woven in each life varies. Some lives have a short string others have a long cord; stretching to many days, months and years.

In spite of their length, not all days and years are equal.

Some are more special than the others; some are pleasant others outlandish. They bring their own blessings and obscenities. However, each blessing and curse shapes and moulds you, leaving a lasting impact in your life. The ebb and flow of life brings and takes people from you...'

You have just read an excerpt from a journal. It belonged to Hamish Mackenzie. His leather bound journal was written for posterity but the account of one specific year was bound and kept with the legal documents of his stately home. Whoever would own this house would have to read his account of that particular year. Here is his message.

'Dear Owner,

Welcome to your new home. You and I are lucky to have called this stone building our earthly abode. I've many memories of this place but one specific year stands taller; it came like no other. Let me take you back to those days.'

Sincerely yours

Hamish Mackenzie

« »

I TURNED 40 A FEW WEEKS ago. They say, it's just a number and I would like to agree with them, whoever 'they' are.

My Chinese friend has sent me a calendar; reminding me that this specific year is the year of the horse. On visiting my Scottish friend, he shows me his calendar, my name, Hamish, written on the day of my birth and my age. That number reminds me that perhaps I have already spent nearly half of my life. Since then I keep thinking that the days of life are slipping away just like my money through my fingers. This fact strikes me like a thunderbolt. I can't decide what is more frightening; losing the coins of my life or not having the coins of the day: the bloody money.

I often wish that I'd learnt at least one proper industry based skill. However, after years of speculating, now I realise that I've a thing for wood. I'm good at working with wood. It speaks to me: a language that's just between the wood and me. The other day, I bid for a big chunk of driftwood. I sliced a circular section of the wood and it spoke to me. I know this piece of wood, once a tree, in its life had adversities; the growth rings are very close, a sign of tough times. It might have been starved due to the lack of food or Mother Nature has ravaged it deliberately.

To me, the driftwood is as if a human battered, shaped and shaved by the storm of life. My heart goes to it as I caress the desolate wood saying, 'I'll make you a dining table, pride of my kitchen, and you'll never starve for food and drink again...that's my promise to you.'

***

AS I SIT IN THIS STATELY HOME, which I inherited from my grandparents, I wonder what they would think of me starting my business within the bounds of this elegant home. I know they strongly believed in keeping the business and work out of the house. To them, a house was a place of rest: a personal corner to be enjoyed and a refuge from the anxieties of the outside world. Both my parents were academics. My grandparents used to say that university uprooted them from their land. They didn't have enough time for anything. I spent my early childhood between the university campus and this stone house of my grandparents.

My grandfather owned a distillery in the heart of the Scottish Highlands, actually not far from this house, and my grandmother was an artist and a housewife. They were two very different people but a perfect match in great harmony: granddad was as open as North Sea but grandma as private as a woodland fairy. I think living in their company, I have become a little like both of them.

I've lived so long in this house that it has become my whole world. I don't want to leave this place. The trouble is I need to get work but not away from this little kingdom of mine. I need money for sure.

My fortune can't sustain. I have enough money to live comfortably for some time, but I know it is neither a jar nor a barrel of Zarepheth's widow that would never run out of oil and flour. Even if I believe, I don't think that I'm lucky enough.

Luck has never been on my side. It's an embarrassment to admit that I have never won even a raffle ticket. I have to be sufficient for myself. Self-reliance has to be my aim if the house has to be my abode for years to come.

Tomorrow, I'll start working on my new project: drift wood, the dining table.

***

I HEAR THE DOORBELL. It's rare to have visitors here unless they are invited. I speculate who would be at my front door. Is it possible that aunt Jean wants to stopover? I spoke to her just last night. She was talking of paying me a visit in one of these days.

With uncertainty, I answer the doorbell. There's a young man, very crisp in every way. As I come out, closing the door behind me, strangely I feel the coolness of a faint water spray on my face. The sky is clear: vast blue over our heads but I wonder.

At first glance, the stranger looks familiar but I don't remember meeting him. For a moment, I forget what to say or ask. He looks much younger than I am, but he commands a very strong presence. My bewildered eyes scan him quickly.

He's wearing trendy denim shorts and a crisp white fine summer shirt. His muscular body is like a seasoned athlete. His long, brown, wavy hair hangs around his neck and shoulders. There's an inky blue-black scar on his right cheek near his ear, which runs down along his neck. A worn out brown leather rucksack hangs on his right shoulder. A pair of walking shoes and a scarf is dangling on both sides.

As I wonder what this fine youth is doing in this far flung area of Highlands, a barking dog behind him decides to be an icebreaker. Soon after, as his smiling eyes fix on my face and his hand extends towards me, he introduces himself,

'I'm Séamus Chisholm'.

I immediately think what a coincidence, a stranger sharing my name only a different version. I try to put a smile on my face as I respond, 'I'm Hamish Mackenzie.'

His dog is making a lot of fuss: running around him and jumping endlessly. Séamus tells me that his dog, Rowan, wants me to pick him up as he has walked for a long time on the winding road.

I lead them to the garden and we take our seats in a sunny spot. Séamus starts talking with ease and confidence. The first thing he says is, 'Well such a huge place and not a horse in sight.'

I wonder what it is with him and horses. He spreads a dog mat on the grass; Rowan sits wagging his tail. He anticipates food. Séamus opens a little can of dog food. The way Séamus looks around seems that he's familiar with the surroundings.

Once he serves and satisfies his dog, he turns towards me,

'Well Hamish, how's your new business?'

I'm pleasantly surprised that he asks me about it. My website 'Beloved Wood' just went live a few days ago. It feels weird that he already seems to know almost everything, which is on the website.

He tells me that he needs a job. Apparently, he's an expert in woodwork and wants to work far from the madding crowds of the city.

My eyes examine his hands. They look smooth. There's no trace of roughness, broken skin or splinter ravaged fingers.

How can he be an expert without carrying the scars of wood? I decide to put him to test so I ask, 'What are you good at?'

'Anything and everything,' he says immediately, and I think what an arrogance.

I'm still thinking that this Greek-god like youth and woodwork don't seem to go together. I guess that his eyes already have seen a suspicion in my look as I'm finding it difficult to trust him.

He asks me for a glass of water and I really feel bad that I haven't offered him a drink. I remember my granddad saying, 'Don't forget to show hospitality to strangers as some unknowingly have entertained angels.' It spurs me to act faster. I lead Séamus to the conservatory. Rowan is happy on the grassy field with his dog bone.

Morag, the housekeeper, has gone to the town, I guess, her car isn't out there. I make Séamus a cup of tea. He looks relaxed as if he's in his element. His sense of familiarity to the surrounding makes me uneasy.

He looks around and smiles. He is scanning the outside through window with a faraway gaze in his eyes. He doesn't say anything; just sips his tea and I feel uncomfortable. I don't know what to say to him. I don't even know him. He's just appeared today from somewhere or nowhere.

Again, he starts. Pointing towards the driftwood in the corner, he says,

'A nice piece...any plan for it.'

I think in my head that this is mine and you've nothing to do with it, but politely I tell him that it's going to be a dining table.

He responds, 'Good choice...drift wood needs to be looked after.'

Now it freaks me out that he can read my thoughts and ideas, but then I calm myself rationalising that maybe he's just a like-minded person. I think, I should put this young arrogant to a test so that he can show me his skill.

I take him downstairs. The workshop is laden with the smell of juniper. It arrived just yesterday. He looks around; loads of wood of all sorts and of course driftwood.

He surveys the wood and my newly done projects. He holds the mirror frame, I carved yesterday, and asks me what he should carve. I immediately tell him, 'A fine horse.'

I don't know why I said 'horse' but I did as if the word was spoken to me. He looks at me in amazement or disappointment. I can't decipher that look. His eyes are shining like a candle in the dark room. I think his eyes are steel blue. He smiles as if he remembers something. Putting the frame down, he says genially,

'Hamish, you've chosen the project. I'll choose the wood.'

He gives me no choice. He just says boldly what he wants to do, and I think maybe there's a likeness of open waters within him. To tell you the truth, I fear that he'd choose the most expensive wood. He wanders around, examining the wood. Now he stands in front of the pine wood section. My immediate thought is that he doesn't even know that this is the cheapest piece in my whole collection of wood. He pulls the logs out and can see the utter shock in my eyes at his choice. I say pointing towards the expensive wood, 'Did you not see the best quality wood?'

He rubs his hands against his denim shorts and says, 'Of course I see your fine wood but...I don't see my fine horse in that wood.'

He seems to be a well-read young man. I'm speechless. He thinks that he's something, but I refuse to believe this champion of words. Words are not enough for me; I don't trade in words. He has to show me his skill by producing this bloody horse now. I show him the tools, and he asks if he can have Rowan with him while he works. I have no objection to that. The little beast is adorable actually. As soon as Séamus puts the dog down, the dog shakes his body and ears as if trying to get rid of water from its fur.

I don't know why I'm still standing here watching him. I feel odd but there's an urge in me to stand and watch. He cuts the wood, organises his tools properly and takes his leave to come tomorrow to carry on his work. He tells me that he's staying in Letterfinlay Lodge near Loch Lochy. As it's a long walk to the Loch, so I offer to drive him down to his lodge; thinking he might be an angel or something. I hope to continue the tradition of my granddad: he was a kind and wise man in his days.

Anyway, Séamus says that he likes walking.

***

MORAG HAS JUST SERVED me evening tea; delicious black pudding. Its taste is still lingering on my lips. My belly is full of niceties of the Highlands, my eyes filled with sleep and my mind with Séamus.

The house is quiet and almost empty.

Stillness has descended on the house. It is summer but the fire is still crackling in the fireplace. The house never gets warm. It needs constant fire. There's cold of ages trapped in its stones. They cry for warmth, endlessly, like a desert for water. I tell you that there's a hunger in them. If I starve them, they will suck every ounce of warmth out of me and mummify me in my own house. I know that stone with snow and ice can be a killer. I worry that I'll not be able to feed the stone house for much longer.

My money is vanishing. I hope my newly started business, which once was my hobby, will help me to heat my house. Its hunger is bigger and deeper than mine is.

Oona, my beloved wife, has gone to Iceland for at least three weeks but I know she'll stay longer. She's still not used to this place. I've spent time here with my grandparents. For the last ten years, I've been a constant presence in this stone house. For Oona, this is fairly new. I think two years would be enough to settle down but not for Oona. She keeps telling me that she misses the mighty mountains and hot water springs of Iceland. She knows her elements as I know mine.

I'm still thinking about Séamus. I hope, he delivers what he claims. It's strange that many people named Séamus and Hamish have lived in this house. My granddad was Hamish, his right hand man in Loch Lochy Distillery was Séamus; and my dad was Séamus. I am Hamish and this stranger is Séamus as well. What is it with this name?

I remember my granddad saying that Séamus, his employee in the distillery, was like a son to him. He trusted him with everything. His money and his whisky barrels were open treasures for him but he never stole any of it. He was a strong man in his mind and body. He worked for my granddad for fifteen years. He was the finest and the fittest person in the distillery. Granddad always said that Séamus never grew weary, as if youth was on his side all the time. People still talk about him. His fellow workers showed signs of aging, wrinkles, crow's feet around their eyes but he was as fresh and young as a new lamb in springtime.

My granddad told me how upset he was when Séamus left the distillery without any sound reason. He just said, 'Too long a service can be emotionally wearing when the time comes to depart.' He took all the actual reasons for leaving with him.

The sun is still lingering in the west. I think that it should go down. Night should descend on the bens, dales and lochs. I want to sleep but the sunlight hangs around, and now the sky is splashed with all the conceivable hues of red, orange and yellow. I think Oona would like this. She keeps singing praises of the sunset on Icelandic mountains.

I stand looking through the window at the endless stretch of green land and blue skies: a blessing to be enjoyed in the Highlands. When the rain descends, every shade of grey grabs the land, mountains and lochs, but even that sight fills me with excitement.

***

I'VE CUT THE WOOD; I have a plan and design in my head and on paper as well for my drift wood sitting in the corner looking at me in anticipation.

Just by cutting the wood and chiselling it, I have minor injuries on my hands already. I guess when I cut the wood it cries and screams. It fears the cruel saw and it takes its revenge by splintering me. I know it will not be like this forever; it will be smooth and polished, and will be proud of its own transformation.

It's unusual for me to work at this time of the night. Morag hears the sound of electric saw. She comes and tells me,

'Don't wake up the wood when it ought to sleep.'

I know she's right. I haven't enjoyed good health for some time now. I need rest.

Morag thinks that the stones of the house and the wood that I have piled up are going to be my enemies. She thinks that I should sell this house and move to the lowlands. Oona agrees with her as well. Sometimes, I feel they gang up on me. However, I feel and somehow believe that the stones of this old house will never grow cold, and the supply of wood and driftwood will never end as long as I am willing to stay.

This house has survived for many countless moons. I'd like to think that resilience is part of its foundation. The look of the stones and the sight of wood, somehow, warms my heart and encourages me to stay.

Especially today, I feel something has changed around the house for good or bad, I don't know yet. 'Beloved Wood' has received attention on the world web, and has brought at least a stranger to my door steps.

Morag brings me a glass of whisky before I go to bed. Only a few bottles of whisky from granddad's distillery are left. These bottles are older than I am. I value every tiny drop and enjoy every little sip of it.

I detach myself from the stone and wood now: the warmth of whisky has hugged me inside out, and I'm in my cosy bed with a hope of a new, happy, better and prosperous tomorrow. I tell myself, 'It's enough for today; tomorrow will look after itself.' But then I think who is going to look after whom tomorrow.

I find myself questioning again. Am I looking after tomorrow or tomorrow is looking after me? I don't have the answer, and I pacify my curious mind by telling myself that it's an old battle between time and man.

**

I WOKE UP THIS MORNING feeling fresh in my body. I have no pain in my arms or legs. However, my mind is as heavy as lead. This feeling makes me tired. I guess, when I was asleep my mind kept a night watch over me and my thoughts. I want to stay longer in my bed, wrapped in crisp white bed linen, but I can't afford to spend extra hours in bed now. I have a fledgling business to tend.

I have to get up. I stretch my legs and I feel the chill in the far end of my bed. In spite of being covered with duvet, that part of the bed is chilled. I think of Oona. She's my hot water bottle. She oozes warmth from every pore of her body.

I'm still in my dressing gown, having a quick walk around the house. Standing in front of the windows and scanning the vast stretch of land, I see Rowan running around but there's no sign of Séamus.

I need to hurry up. My potential employee seems to be efficient. I guess Morag has taken care of Séamus. She's fantastic and fanatic about looking after strangers. She has never told me her reason for doing so.

Yes, I was right. As I come downstairs, Séamus is sitting with Morag. She's served him breakfast. She laughs and tells me what Séamus says.

He has told her that he can smell water from a distance; and she makes fun of him saying that it isn't just water but the fire water which he smells. I know by firewater she means Loch Lochy Whisky but I don't think Séamus understands. I have an endless thirst for Lochy, but at the moment the smell of coffee has already filled my nostrils and my taste buds are already impatient to be drowned in this hot brown drink.

Séamus stands up to greet me. I notice; he's very tall but I'm not a midget either. Again, I feel a faint chill of water spray on my face, and I wipe it with a tissue but there is no trace of dampness. It just feels weird.

As I hold his soft hand in my hand, I wonder if he's going to impress or disappoint me. My feeling is for the latter. From my experience, the hands of the wood worker speak before he even opens his mouth. In this case, Séamus's hands don't endorse the story he tells.

As Morag gets my breakfast ready, Séamus goes to start his work. He takes Rowan with him downstairs. I tell him that Morag has lit the fire so it will be warm. But he doesn't seem to care about fire.

Serving me breakfast, Morag says that the poor man seems to be desperate to get work. I share my suspicions about his skill and I ask Morag if she thinks he'd be good in woodwork. She shakes her head in negation. I hope my doubts have not influenced her view, nevertheless, I find comfort that her opinion is the same as mine.

I've nearly finished my breakfast. I'm going to work on my driftwood table. I feel as if I'm in a competition and have to finish it before Séamus but also it has to be a piece of art. So I leave in hurry.

I'm working upstairs because it's sunny here. I need as much heat as this stone house. Oona doesn't approve of me working upstairs. The sawdust gets everywhere, she says. However, I think it will be fine today.

I've just set my worktable and tools right, and I can't ignore that Rowan is moaning constantly. I never owned a dog so I don't understand dog language. It begins to annoy me: it's too much noise and I don't like being disturbed. Morag runs to me with the news that Rowan has a splinter in his paw and Séamus wants to leave to care for him.

I think it's the end of the beginning for any job prospect for Séamus. A part of me thinks that perhaps he's making excuses. I guess he's aware that I need my business to get going, and he hopes to get the job anyway without giving me the finished product. I need another worker but I can't afford an experimental employee.

Morag informs me that he wants to come tomorrow. I tell Morag that she can decide when he should come. It's her who has to deal with the early morning visitors.

My potential employee has left even before the mid-day. I know in my heart that he isn't going to survive this test but still it disappoints me that he's gone.

***

IT'S A BEAUTIFUL DAY, Oona would say that I should be out in the glens and dales enjoying my heritage. It's a good idea but I've put myself in a competition, and the driftwood is crying to be alleviated into a table. I know I'll be better in delivering my end product even though I don't claim to be an expert like Séamus. His hands and choice of wood is enough data for me to process and formulate my opinion about his product.

I've taken a simple approach this time. I don't dare to cut any more of this torn away driftwood thinking that it has already experienced too many bruises. It's naturally a nicely shaped piece as if pillars are standing together. I decide to use glass for the table top, surrounded by the driftwood, which will also form the centre of the table. The glass will not hide the charm of this torn apart beauty and the wooden part under the table top will hold bread, wine, water and what not as it has been promised.

I feel tired now so I decide to go out. The day is truly charming. I ask Morag to accompany me. She jumps into my car. We don't use this car very often. It's expensive to run when we have to run and feed a giant stone house too. Therefore, it's a special trip. Every drop of fossil fuel matters.

We drive through serpent-like winding roads. Our conversation is varied: ranging from weather to Séamus, from Rowan to ravens gathered in enormous numbers in a nearby field.

I decide to ask Morag why she is kind to strangers. She says that it's our human obligation but she also adds that her grandfather told them about a wanderer. I'm not aware of any wanderer so I'm all ears as she continues,

'The story goes that a wanderer called Fraser roamed the glens in the past. No one knew who he was. He would come and go every now and then but sometimes he disappeared for months...He'd ask for food and shelter. Sometimes, he'd spend the night in the farm with animals. People have seen him sleeping beside sheep during snow. Some people say that horses were scared of Fraser and he wasn't comfortable around them either...But many said that his presence blessed them in some ways. People claimed that he touched the animals and they were healed. He could run like the wind and snatched the lambs from foxes. People also talk that he blessed the waters of Lochs. Some even say that he blessed the peat and heather on the hills too. Many have witnessed an unusual and untimely flourishing and thriving of heather on the hills.'

I don't have faith in these folklores but I've started this conversation, so now I have to be polite and listen without being too opinionated.

Morag continues saying, 'My mum says that there are stories of another wanderer too, called Duncan. But I don't know how true they are. I've never had an encounter with any wanderer...However, I believe that myths don't come from nowhere; I'd like to think that they have their origin in some sort of reality...and we all know that reality can be distorted. Time is a game changer. It plays Chinese whispers with us...don't you think.'

I still don't want to believe in these myths but the conviction with which she speaks spurs me to be open minded, and try to understand the things that are beyond the realm of my scientific inquiry.

I ask her if she knows anything of his appearance. Morag isn't sure but she's heard that he was always dressed in a nice kilt. There are stories about his handsomeness and how young women were attracted to him but he was a wanderer, who never stayed long enough anywhere.

She further continues, 'I remember this story that on one stormy night, this wanderer asked for shelter. The woman of the house was spinning wool. In return for a hot meal and a blanket to sleep in, he helped the woman to spin the wool...and guess what?...In the morning when she woke up, the wanderer was gone...but her basket was full of spun wool.'

It's fascinating to listen to Morag. I've never had a detailed discussion on any specific topic with her before but now I know why, when Oona and Morag go out they forget about time. She's a chatterbox. I'm not complaining. I'm thoroughly enjoying listening to her, even though I don't believe in any of these stories.

Now, we stop in front of the main entrance of the local distillery. I whisper Lochy and Morag looks at me. I tell her that it used to be my granddad's distillery. I wonder, how bad things were that he had to sell his thriving business. I've been living in this area for a while but I've never tasted whisky from this distillery. They've changed the name of the distillery but the old horse statue still sits at the main entrance. It's a piece of art and knowing my granddad as an art lover; I wonder why he left it there. Perhaps it fetched good money, I tell myself.

I've no desire to go and see the distillery, which my granddad worked hard for with his blood and sweat and now someone else is reaping the benefit of those hard times. But Morag disagrees with me. She says,

'If you want to remember and honour the efforts of your granddad then you must go in. It still carries his mark, the horse.'

She speaks convincingly and I'm annoyed that this young woman almost half of my age, has the power to persuade me.

We walk into the distillery and I introduce myself. The old gentleman immediately recognises me. He tells me that he joined the distillery just one month before it was sold. He's pleased that someone from Mackenzie's has come to the distillery. He shows us around and thinks that Morag is my daughter. He keeps telling her how fine and kind a man her great granddad was. When we leave, he hands me a whisky bottle as a token of thanks to my granddad. He was the last man hired by my granddad before the business went down.

***

IN THE EVENING, MORAG serves delicious steak. I think, she's the best steak maker. No one does my steak the way I like it done. Somehow, she knows and does it perfectly every single time. I believe, she will be a fine chef one of these days. I'm sad that her work is going to end with us soon.

She came to us some months ago. She needed money to fund her training course. She offered her cooking skills and we paid her for this in addition to providing her lodging. She has become like a family member. She was teasing me when she served me the whisky from the distillery, 'Dad, here is your firewater.' She doesn't like whisky but I'm glad because I can enjoy it all by myself. Oona thinks, it stinks and I say that's fine.

I appreciate the old man's thought to give me a bottle from the distillery that my granddad had established but I hate to say that I don't like it. For me, it isn't rounded enough. It seems a bit shallow. I don't feel the depth of its taste. Even my nose doesn't approve the fumes of it. I feel awful to have this bad analysis of their whisky. One would suppose that it is definitely my prejudice otherwise there's nothing wrong with the whisky. I'm happy with my Lochy bottles. It makes me sad that they aren't going to last very long. I believe that Lochy is the best whisky, the world has ever produced.

After having that watered down version, I pour the real McCoy: Lochy, beautiful golden yellow liquid, for myself and I raise the glass to the 'horse' outside the distillery, the only presence of granddad's business. It has warmed me inside out, as it always does.

***

I GET UP NEXT MORNING to find out that I've overslept. Morag didn't bother to wake me up. Normally if I'm late, she checks on me and brings me coffee. I feel annoyed, not at her but at myself. It is nearly 11:30 am.

I know that my driftwood is waiting for me and I'm sure that Séamus has already started working. I think, he wouldn't be able to complete it because it's a huge project that I've given him. He has three days to finish it. I guess he's chatting with Morag and it will delay his work progress. They both seem to be chatterboxes. Good for them.

I come downstairs to find Morag sleeping in the conservatory, in the beautiful golden sunshine. It's unusual for her to be asleep at this time of the day. I don't want to disturb her. I'll get some brunch sorted out for myself but before I do anything, I need to see my potential employee busy in my workshop.

As I step down and turn the light on; I see that there's a sign on the door, written with coal on brown paper 'Do not disturb, please.' A huge shock to me, undoubtedly. It feels as if Séamus has already claimed his work place. How can he do this without my approval? I have to see his work first. I knock at the door and he slips a note through the door: 'Not now.'

I'm astonished at the blatant boldness of this young man. I don't know what to do. I leave for the kitchen. As I fill the kettle, Morag enters apologising for not having my meal ready. She tells me that Séamus was at the door at 5:00 am. She served him breakfast and since then he is working.

She asks me if I felt chilled when I was around Séamus yesterday. I felt faint water spray but I don't want her to get frightened so I lie to her. She says that the back of his chair was ice cold when he left for the workshop. She adds that when he walks it feels as if damp breeze comes from him. I tell her that there's nothing to worry about, the house is normally very cold but she isn't convinced.

Morag's going down the hill today for groceries in the local shops. We buy local produce especially milk, eggs and meat. Oona has taken a shine to venison recently and having a cook like Morag, you are good to have fine, sophisticated and luxurious dinners.

I phone Oona. She tells me that she was browsing through 'Beloved Wood' and there are lots of comments and compliments on different products by somebody called Séamus.

To her surprise, I tell her that he's already here in the house and carving pinewood. She's happy that someone has come in response to our live website. But I tell her not to be very excited and hopeful as the guy is posh with soft hands, and I wonder if he can do much to impress me.

She tells me that I have to be patient and wait for his finished product. She also informs me that she's collected some interesting pieces of driftwood for me, and she already knows what she wants me to do with it.

It was wonderful to speak to Oona. I miss her. She's in a strange situation. When she's here she misses Iceland and when she's there she misses Scotland. I guess, I've lived all my days in Scotland so I don't understand the complex feelings of home and belonging. She tells me that she might come sooner than she planned. I encourage her to stay and enjoy because I know when she's back she will pine for Iceland.

She has also told me that she's coming back with an excellent idea for her own little business, which somehow frightens me. Her creative and fertile mind spins up ideas sometimes very outlandish to me. However, I'm pleased because we both want to keep this house. Business mind set is a bonus. She knows how important this house is to me.

***

I HEAR A NOISE DOWNSTAIRS. It must be Séamus, and yes, he's out now. He looks at me and raises his hat to say, hi. He says that no one is allowed to see his unfinished project yet. He tells me that he's hungry and needs to feed himself. He's ready to go but I don't want him to leave without me offering him something from my own kitchen.

I tell him that Morag is out so he has to help himself in the kitchen. I welcome him to use my kitchen and everything that is there. He lets Rowan go out in the grassy field surrounded by the dyke.

I take out eggs from the fridge and it seems that the expiry date on them has passed two days ago. I warn him and he says, 'Before 1950, the date on food simply didn't exist. We had to rely on our nose and eyes. I'm sure these eggs are perfectly fine.'

He cracks the eggs in the bowl and I think he doesn't look that old to know about 1950s. To me, he's in his late twenties. I wonder how he can talk about the time, he has not lived in, with so much certainty.

I'm still looking at his hands: smooth like a baby's bottom. With his side-glance, he's aware that I'm watching him. He looks through the window not saying anything. I break the silence,

'This is the most beautiful part of the world. I've lived here for nearly twenty years off and on. I can't get enough of it.'

He nods, without looking towards me he says,

'I agree. Even if you live a thousand years in these glens and dales, your senses will never grow tired.'

I can't help thinking that there's a kind of ancient wisdom and patience in his eyes and the tone of his voice is unbelievably mellow.

As soon as Séamus finishes, his rustically put together meal, he wants to resume his work. I offer him tea and he stays hesitantly. He asks of my driftwood table and that reminds me that I haven't worked on it today at all. I need to speed up my efforts. I wink as I respond to him,

'Work is in progress and no one is allowed to eye my unfinished project.'

He understands the punch in my voice and his mouth widens in a full hearty smile. Then he asks of my long term business plan. I tell him that we need to start some kind of business here otherwise, I can't afford to live in this house.

'So what's your plan?' he asks me again.

I don't want to share my ideas and plans with a stranger, I just met so I change the subject, 'That discussion is for another day. Let's get back to our work.'

On descending the stairs he says, 'I'll show you my horse only when you show me your table.'

Without waiting for my response, he closes the door behind him. He seems to be a word athlete and doesn't accept defeat very easily. I feel, he's challenged me and I need to respond to it.

I get back to my project. I know mine is very simple as compared to Séamus's horse but I don't have to prove my skill. I'm just keeping the promise to restore the badly battered driftwood but I need to enhance the beauty of my simple wood and glass.

I'm extremely tired. Wood battles with you and sucks out your energy. I wonder how Séamus is getting on with the pinewood. I'm nearly finished, sawdust is everywhere. I sigh with relief when I finally put the glass on the top and screw it to the wood. I dust it out. The wood looks brighter as if smiling on its fortune. I don't think polish is needed just now.

As I put my tools in the bag, I hear someone coming upstairs. It is Séamus with Rowan on his shoulders; ready to leave, telling me that his horse is finished and he needs to leave. I tell him that my table is ready as well.

'So let's reveal them,' he says and his steel blue eyes shine, smile and pry my facial expression.

I suggest putting our projects downstairs.

He has moved his horse. I've no idea of its scale. He tells me that I should come with my table now. He gives me space to move. I set my table. He's covered his horse with rags from my workshop. I am shocked. It is enormous in size. I don't know how he has moved it out single-handed. He's a young man but not a giant, and Rowan is no help to him. He has just surprised me again.

We stand beside our covered projects.

I ask him to reveal his horse. He pulls the cover and I see a huge black stallion. I can't believe my eyes. I'm shockingly surprised and lost for words. I could have not imagined that pinewood will lend itself to be carved into such a beauty in a short period of time.

He has also polished it. I'm astonished. I go near and touch its mane, ears, and beautiful tactile tail. It reminds me of the pewter horse outside the distillery. This is a masterpiece as well. It is a slap to my arrogant judgement based on his hands and choice of wood.

Curiously, he asks me why I asked him for a horse.

I say, 'Your first comment was about horses.'

He nods and shrugs.

Now, it's my turn and mine is nothing like his. It's simple and clean but more importantly, it is restored. He moves closer and I remove the cover.

He smiles, sits on the floor and touches the wood, the glass and then shakes my hand saying, 'Nice, indeed very nice.' I don't know if he is impressed or what but I am, extremely. I pull two chairs around the table saying, 'Let me keep my promise.'

He takes his seat and I bring a decanter half filled with whisky. I put it on the table saying, 'I give you golden warm liquid, and you will enjoy the company of this decanter.'

I've fulfilled my promise: the drink is on the drift wood table. It will not starve for warmth or company any more. It has me, at least, as long as I'm alive and Lochy, as long as it lasts. Not a bad company at all.

We raise the glass weirdly to the horse. Séamus smiles and tells me that he loves the dram of gods. As soon as he lifts the glass to his nostrils he says, 'Lochy'.

I stare at him in disbelief. The bottle of Loch Lochy is older than Séamus. The world has not seen Loch Lochy for a long time. How does he recognise this whisky? He has given me a shock of my life; the decanter nearly slipped from my hand. I can't but ask him, 'How do you know about Loch Lochy.'

He sips a mouthful and after a while without looking at me his response is, 'How could I not.'

To be honest, I am a bit edgy though not scared. He asks for more. He clearly likes it. He totally ignores my shock at his familiarity of the flavour of Lochy and asks if I am willing to give him a job now. He wants to know my decision by tomorrow. He leaves his address with me.

I'm astonished at his craftsmanship thinking that I'm ready to take apprenticeship with him. In my eyes, he's a master artist but he is humble and down to earth.

The summer sun is still shining and I watch him going down the road. He runs with Rowan and looks back once. I think he's aware that I'm watching him.

I find it difficult to pose probing questions to him. There's something about him that stops me being open and bold. I have no idea who he is. A thought crosses my mind who knows if he is an angel or a wanderer. The latter option is unlikely because he's neither a Fraser nor a Duncan.

Back in the room, I look at the horse and I can't help thinking it is magical. I'm amazed and I wonder if he can do this with the pinewood then what will be the outcome of him laying his hands on my finest wood.

It feels as if he's more than one person; he does it so fast that I feel ashamed to think that for my table I took as long as he did for his marvellous horse.

In spite of all the questions that I want to ask him, I'm definitely going to give him this job. I hope fortune has knocked at my door.

Whoever Séamus is, he fascinates me. There's something complex and mysterious about him. Knowing that I know nothing about him, intrigues me even more.

***

MORNING LIGHT TICKLES ME. I open my eyes. I had a dream, seeing the horse galloping in the house and eventually running out in the field.

I put on my dressing gown and immediately go downstairs to check on the horse. To my relief, it's still there where Séamus left it last night with all its might and beauty, commanding a very strong presence just like its maker.

Morag is serving me breakfast and she tells me how surprised she is to see the horse. She confesses that she didn't see something like that coming from Séamus, the posh kind as he appears. We both share the embarrassment of our judgement of his skill based on trivial attributes of his physique and personality.

Morag fills me with all the news of the town. She also informs me, what else she has heard about the wanderer from an old woman who she had a conversation with over lunch just the day before in the village.

She's surprised to find out that the wanderer has not always been good. He had a dark side to him as well. She tells me that the wanderer has been known to steal things from homes. Once he was caught stealing eggs and bread. He was about to be flogged when he broke open the chains, he was tied with and left.

She continues another story, 'During a stormy night, he asked for shelter and the next morning he disappeared stealing the newly made kilt and a tartan blanket, which was for the chieftain of the clan.'

I think Morag seems to have developed a fascination for the wanderer. She's digging in. In some ways, she is like me: curious and inquisitive.

I think if I have a daughter, probably, I'd like her to be somewhat like Morag. Just like her to have a hunger and thirst for knowing and exploring.

***

BEFORE I LEAVE THE HOUSE to see Séamus at his lodge by Loch, Lochy, I phone Oona. She's surprised at what I tell her but she's even more taken aback that I have decided to give him lodging at the house as well. She doesn't say anything. I know she's sceptical but once she sees his work she will be convinced.

I put my suit on. I want to look like a boss. My pointy shoes are shiny. I don't particularly like them but Oona says they are trendy. She thinks, I live in another time and world. I'm not bothered with what's trendy and what isn't. As long as my house is warm, there's bread and wine on my table and Oona to love me, I am perfectly fine.

I make sure the letter is in my pocket before I start the car engine. I follow the address and find Séamus sitting outside. His eyes are behind the binoculars. He's surveying Loch Lochy. It's chilly. He's in his fine kilt without wearing heavy outdoor clothes.

He is unaware of my presence. I clear my throat as I say, 'Any fascination in the Loch.'

He is startled; he nearly drops his binocular and I feel embarrassed of my verbal ambush. He lets the binocular hang around his neck and stands up to shake hands with me. I feel his hands are ice cold. He says in his mellow voice, 'All the fascination of life is here...in this Loch.'

I have no clue what allures him in the Loch. But I tell you that he's a champion of words. Whenever he opens his mouth, he makes me speechless.

I feel cold so Séamus leads me in. He puts the kettle on saying, 'I hope the horse hasn't come back to life.'

I nearly jumped. He's startled me. It was my dream about the horse. I wonder how come he gets the wind of it. I put a nervous smile on display, 'No, he isn't. If he comes back to life then I'll chain him forever; such a beauty can't leave.'

'Forever...is a dangerous word...To hold on to something forever is neither good for the object nor for the captor.'

What is he trying to reveal? I seem to be utterly incapable of the riddles he throws my way. I take out the white crisp envelope and extend it towards him.

He reads it, smiling and nodding as if he was already sure that the job was his. He simply says 'Thank you,' and shakes my hand. He makes me a cup of coffee. I must say that it's a perfect cup of coffee: intense aroma, full bodied and creamy in my mouth.

I offer him lodging and he looks and sounds pleased. He tells me that the lodge he lives in eats his money like termites voraciously feast on the wood. I know exactly how he feels. My stone house does the same thing with me. I guess he's aware that my house is a stone building. In the warmth of his lodge, I feel that I must inform him about the perpetual cold that resides in my house needing constant fire especially during winter.

He doesn't seem to be bothered and shrugging his shoulders says, 'I'm never cold.' A very sure and immediate response leaves me nothing to say.

After a few moments of silence, Séamus lifts his head. Squeezing his eyes, full of a brazen look, he inquires if there is small print to be read for this job offer.

I immediately say, 'There will be no secrets between us.'

He swirls the remaining coffee in his mug and shakes his head in affirmation.

'Anything you want to say,' I continue.

He looks at me, 'I'm a free spirit and I want to be free in my work and choices.'

I have no objection to his fundamental right of freedom but I tell you he's strong and capable to fight with his tongue, lashing out heavy strikes of words.

Séamus tells me that he's ready to move today. I didn't expect this, but I immediately phone Morag to get the guest room ready for Séamus thinking later we'll sort out his proper room. Morag sounds grumpy over this sudden news. She's a nice girl but sometimes has a mind of her own. Anyway, she promises that it will be ready by evening.

I'm astonished, Séamus has very little belongings. He has two rucksacks and Rowan to bring with him. I actually had forgotten about Rowan. Oona isn't a dog person but I've made the offer and we'll make it work, hopefully. She's flexible I know that for sure.

Séamus locks the lodge, returns the key, and with a final look at the Loch, he follows me.

Rowan seems more excited than Séamus.

***

I TAKE SÉAMUS TO THE guest room. The fire is lit already but a dense chill still hangs in the room. I'm pleased that there's an extra warm blanket on the bed too. I just feel that I need to look after this young man. Not because he is my employee now, but also that it was important to my grandparents to look after strangers. There's still a wooden plaque in the visitor's room, where the quote about strangers reminds me about my role in nurturing fellow humans.

To be honest, I'm a little apprehensive that things have happened so quickly and I've been quite abrupt in my decision-making. I don't even know where he comes from. But I hope all goes well with all of us under this roof.

Séamus puts his bags on the floor and looks around with a strange familiarity in his eyes. It seems, he knows something about the house. He looks around as if searching for something. I'm asking myself if he's been here before. Perhaps he reads my eyes and immediately asks where the place is for Rowan. I say that we can put him in the small room for the night.

As we go downstairs, he looks at the huge portraits of my grandparents, my father and aunt Jean when she was young. He stops in front of granddad's portrait and I feel as if he has a wordless chat with him. Then he stands in front of aunt Jeans portrait; I'm sure he's taken aback by her beauty. I notice that his eyes are fixed on her necklace and his hand moves to his own neck. I can see a silver chain around his neck.

He admires the artwork. He seems to be a very cultured man. He asks me where my portrait is and I respond, 'My grandmother couldn't do that in her later years, she lost her eyesight...and it's a hobby of posh people to get their portraits done. I'll go down without a portrait and that's fine.'

Séamus seems to be at home. We decide to go to our workshop.

I sit behind my big table and he wanders around looking at the little projects done by me. I invite him to take seat for a proper chat as my employee. He seems to be excited and a little impatient. He wants to get started as soon as possible.

I tell him that my initial plan is to make some sample wooden art pieces, put them on the website, and later take orders for commissioned items as well. Once we have it going, then we move towards bespoke commissioned furniture. He nods, biting his lips and running his hand through his long wavy hair. I know it is difficult to build up our clientele but I have to start somewhere. He listens to me carefully; his eyes show that he's processing information very fast.

We decide on our initial project: to make some decorative pieces. I leave it to him, as I know he wants freedom in his work. To mark the start of our business day, although it is late afternoon, I pour us some whisky. He looks at me with a big smile as he has his first sip, 'It's not from the same bottle as yesterday.'

And I know, he is spot on. I respond to his contagious smile, 'You have a very fine palate young man.'

On my questioning, he tells me that he was given some bottles and he remembers the taste. I think he must have known somebody or be related to someone who worked at Loch Lochy but I just leave it there; no further questioning. I don't want to be too personal today. I have a lot to ask him but not just today.

I couldn't keep Lochy away from him and from myself too. He is building up my curiosity as we continue with few more rounds of sipping Lochy.

***

IT IS AN UNPLANNED SPECIAL evening; I wish Oona could join us. I miss her but we must offer a proper welcome meal to Séamus tonight. Morag's busy in the kitchen. She wants to shine, I guess. She has planned the meal, and I know she will execute it well. I'm already feeling elated.

Morag invites us into the dining hall. I'm pleased that we can still entertain in the tradition of my grandparents.

Morag has fed us lamb tonight and it's absolutely delicious. The phone rings and it is Oona. Morag and Séamus carry on their meal and chat. As I leave the table, their conversation somehow has turned towards coffee and he tells her that there are 1000 chemical compounds in the coffee, out of which 800 are aromatic compounds. She wonders how an ordinary wood worker knows the chemistry of food. She suspects that he has a degree in chemistry but he simply denies. I know she doesn't believe him.

When I come back to the table, Morag's startled at what she just heard. She tells me with some kind of secrecy in the tone of her voice, 'Séamus says that he is a wanderer.'

My immediate response is, 'But he's not a Fraser.'

I know, I haven't satisfied her but I note that Séamus has picked up a faint scent of some suspicion in our conversation. He immediately says,

'I guess, I'm a lexophile; and at my age it's inevitable not to develop a taste for fine words.'

He explains simply that he's a traveller and wants to live in the Highlands and that's why he looks for work in this area.

There is a sense of apprehension on Morag's face. She asks him, 'So where are you originally from?'

I can guess Séamus doesn't like being questioned; nevertheless he answers, 'Not far from here but...I'm homeless. I fell out with my family.'

Silence drops like a heavy curtain, so this is the end of our conversation. We sit for a while without speaking.

Now as there is no spoken language in action to give focus to my thoughts, so I find myself concentrating on what I'm chewing, and then the ingredients of Morag's naked salad: the most unessential item on the table which she thinks is pivotal for the life of a meal and its receivers.

We are still in this silence struck moment, and I suddenly remember what people say when a sudden silence drops during a lively conversation. It is said that angels pass through your doors. I'm not sure about this and I go with the quietness.

Morag doesn't ask any further personal questions but I know she's inquisitive just like me. Later when she serves dessert, she sets the trajectory of our conversation away from his life and asks, 'Have you heard of the Highland wanderer?'

He takes a spoonful and responds, 'Of course, I have...Who hasn't in the Highlands?'

She tells him the same stories, she told me the other day.

He says that there are many stories that are not simply correct. I wonder how he could be so self-assured in saying so. If I were asked this question, I'd have said that I don't believe in them rather than declaring that they are incorrect. How does he know the status and degree of their correctness or in-correctness?

Séamus continues, 'There must be some truth in them; but I suspect it has been distorted over time...Time has a terrible habit of twisting and bending many things.'

I think he's quite right, something I completely agree with.

It's the longest time, for a long time, that we're still sitting around the dining table even after we've finished our meal. I like it.

The house seems to be alive, fuller and warmer. I guess stones get tired of seeing the same faces day in and out.

Séamus asks me about my wife and I give him a synopsis saying that he would meet Oona soon. He doesn't ask further. He looks at Morag with a half-smile as if he's about to say something but no, he doesn't say a word. I find his half-smile mystifying and ambiguous. I think, he wants to know about Morag.

I'm older than perhaps both of their ages combined so I feel comfortable just watching the young people interacting in a wordless language.

***

I'M SITTING FOR MY BREAKFAST. Morag always comes with food and news. She tells me that Séamus hasn't slept in the guest room last night. I can't decide if she's complaining or hinting some suspicions. I'm sure that he's cold there. She tells me that she found him sleeping on the floor hugging his dog. We both think that he's too much attached to his dog.

I need to think about the lodging for his dog next to him. I don't know which room Oona would like Séamus to be in so I think, he should have his dog with him in the guest room.

Morag tells me that he's been working straight after he woke up. His diligence to work inspires and motivates me. I will go down to the workshop soon after I've finished my breakfast. Meanwhile, Morag asks me what I think of him.

To me, he's an interesting and likeable person but a bit mysterious especially what he says is riddles, most of the time.

I guess, she's quite taken aback by his craftsmanship and off course his handsomeness. I think young women would have fallen at his feet wherever he was, before coming here. I also feel sorry that he has had a rough time being homeless.

Morag thinks that he's a catch but she worries that he's up to something and that we should keep an eye on him. What I like about Morag is that she isn't just a cook at our house. She genuinely cares for Oona, the house and me. I assure her that all will be fine.

I leave for downstairs. On turning the light on in our workshop, I'm up for a surprise. There's a beautifully carved name of my company 'Beloved Wood' hanging on the big heavy door. I'm pleasantly surprised and genuinely pleased. I knock at the door; no response so again I tap my fingers. I think he isn't in there. I open the door, and I can't tell you how shocked I am.

There's a row of newly finished projects, which aren't mine but his. He clearly hasn't slept the whole night. But how can he do all this by himself in one night unless he has got help from pixies.

Honestly, I can't believe my eyes.

For a moment, it feels as if I'm dreaming. To further my shock, he's carved another black horse smaller than the one he's done for me the other day. There's a little price tag on it saying, 'SOLD' and its price £800 underneath. I find on the table the exact amount of the price for that horse.

I'm gobsmacked. I need to see him. I rush upstairs; he isn't in his room. I find him outside at the back of the house standing in front of our old garage. Rowan barks and he knows that they aren't alone any more. He comes round and greets me saying, 'What a potential in this building, let's not waste it.'

It seems, he already has a plan. I immediately think that he's an employee just a few days old in this job and he's already acting like a partner. The self-assurance in his tone bothers me. He hasn't given me a chance to say anything about the shock he's given me in my workshop.

I put on a smile, it isn't essential but it makes me feel good and will hide my bewilderment. I ask, 'Did we talk about the night shift...I mean your work.'

He cracks his knuckles saying, 'No of course not but...We talked about my freedom.'

I think, he has a point. I'm not angry but I'm desperate to know how he has done this. I say, 'Did you have help from someone else?'

He has this smug smile spread on his face and even in his eyes, 'Do you think Rowan has artistic paws or Morag the patience to work all night?'

He makes me laugh, 'It seems as if I've employed ten people in one.'

He responds, 'It's not a bad estimate.'

I tell you, he likes verbal punching.

As we both rest our backs on the cold dyke that surrounds my estate, he looks around. He shows interest in the old garage. Apart from our old ford, I can't even remember what else is in there. He changes the subject,

'How big is your dream about your business?'

I stretch my arms behind my back, 'Very big.'

He smiles, 'Then let me help you, I've come to do so.'

I thank him for his good heart but I don't understand that a person who appeared so desperate to get a job, now says that he is there to help me. I'm not being cynical but just surprised the way this young man is unfolding himself.

I begin to like him. He feels good for me. He excites me, energises me and makes me think big. I can't help thinking, he is god sent.

He is ready to leave to get his work started again. I feel that he's always in hurry. He wants to get things done at an enormous rate even though I haven't given him any deadline for anything.

***

EVERYBODY IS ASLEEP INCLUDING Rowan; I've not heard him barking, and I guess he's satisfied being close to Séamus. A thought crosses my mind; I should make a proper small kennel for Rowan and I like this thought. It is a kind thing to do.

I put the £800 in my safe and wonder who has Séamus bought the horse for. It's a big and expensive gift. He hasn't told me and I've not asked him. I notice that he's taken the small black stallion with him.

I'm working on my website. I discussed the prices of items with Séamus earlier, now I've taken photos, and my website is updated: new items with their photos. It seems that my business has taken small baby steps on the world web.

I look around; Séamus has carved things so fast that I think, I need to move our finished products in another room.

There's another row of new items that he's added during the day. He's already gone to bed early today. I guess he's tired.

Morag wasn't around for tea, so it's been a comparatively quiet evening.

***

TODAY, SÉAMUS HAS LEFT a note on the dining table that he wants to have a business meeting. I'm not sure what is to be discussed. It seems that inadvertently we're becoming business partners. I think perhaps I'll be taking the business and retail side of it and Séamus as a master crafter.

It's afternoon and I've not seen Séamus since morning but I know, he'll be around soon for the meeting. I'm waiting in the conservatory. I can see the whole estate stretched in front of me. The vastness isn't too empty today. I guess, when your heart has hope, it changes the outlook of anything and everything around you.

Séamus has just arrived followed by Rowan. I'm amused and say, 'I wasn't informed that a third member is invited as well.'

He smiles and in a similar manner says,

'Don't worry, he's on mute.'

We both have a good laugh.

He says that he wants to see the garage and secondly, he tells me that he wants his wage in cash. This is first part of the meeting; second will take place in front of or inside the garage.

After some difficulty, I manage to find the key, and I follow Séamus. He's already at the entrance of the garage. I unlock the door, and it opens with a big moan as if we woke it from a deep slumber. It's a stone building as well. It used to be many things. Now it is storage.

He proposes to tidy it up, work on it and make it a proper place to store our finished products here. It's a good idea but it will require a lot of money. Many things have to be changed and put together from scratch. The floor is the big project, and then double glazed windows if it has to be properly used as a living business place.

I frankly tell him that I'll wait for a few weeks to see how the website and sale goes and then I'll be able to invest in it. He says that it's fair enough. He also assures me that he'll be ready to contribute money in case. I'm touched by his generosity. He looks at the Caravan, an old-fashioned one. He peeps through the windows and he winks.

To be honest, he's half of my age but I feel comfortable that he's taking the lead. I have apprehensions but my trust in him is slightly more than my inner nervousness.

***

AGAIN, I'M AMAZED TO SEE the amount of projects he's finished today. I'm sure that we need to do something sooner if the pace of his work continues.

Now it's my job to take photos of any new items, and change the quantity of items available on the website for every single item.

I guess I should also check if there are any orders. I'd be pleased if there are even a few orders, as it is just the start. I find myself praying, 'Please don't disappoint me.'

I nearly jump; 20 orders are waiting to be processed and dispatched. I can't believe my eyes. I need to do something with these orders; photos for new items can wait until tomorrow.

I open the cupboard and take out envelopes, bubble wraps, tape, glue etc. I'm so excited. Believe me or not my eyes are welled up, my legs are shaking, my mind is thinking, and forcing me to pack the orders faster than my hands can cope. I wish I could borrow arms from an octopus today. It's going to be a long night for me.

I think, Oona needs to know about all this excitement now. But unfortunately, the wall clock tells me it's bit too late. She must be asleep. I know, she'll be over the moon. I hope she can find a place in her heart for Rowan. It worries me because Séamus cares for this little dog more than anything else.

Now the orders are packed and ready to be dispatched. They're sitting in the dispatch basket, warming my heart as the gifts under the Christmas tree did, when I was a child. If I could issue a decree, I'd have called this night to be celebrated as 'night of fortune'. I decide to celebrate this moment. I light a candle and pour a glass of Lochy; companion of my nights. With Lochy I'm never alone.

I'm incredibly tired but the thrill of hope has stolen my sleep. As I prepare to leave, the whole workshop seems alive. The fire in the corner is dying but the amber of its blaze is still glowing in the semi dark room. It looks a magical place not a part of my cold stone house. It seems as if I'm standing in the workshop of a skilled elf.

This place has amazed me so much in the last few days. I hope it continues to do so.

I bless Séamus's heart and his timely arrival at this house.

***

I'M AWAKE SINCE GOD knows when, but I don't want to stir the household at this ungodly hour of the morning. I run the list of things to do in my head, and at the top of the list is the first run to the local post office.

There's a freshness in my whole being; my legs and arms seem to rejuvenate, and there's no pain and unease in them. The birds are chirping merry and joyous, and my bed can't contain me anymore.

I get myself ready.

To my surprise, downstairs is already awake; washing machine is running in the kitchen. I can hear the kettle roaring, and I wonder what is happening to this house.

Morag is emptying the dishwasher. She is surprised; her eyes wide open and jaws drop. I see this quizzical look in her eyes. As I pour a mug of hot water, she takes me to the dining hall to show me something magical.

I'm seriously surprised and quizzical too. There's a beautiful black stallion, sitting next to Morag's chair. It has a message hanging around its neck on a small wooden piece: 'To the lady who satisfies the ageless hunger of mine; May your ride of life be smooth.'

She clearly is stunned and she says,

'Why would he do that?' and I think in my heart don't be thick; you're beautiful and he's young and charming. I tell her to value the stallion; people aren't showered with such luxurious and magical gifts every day.

I ask Morag if Séamus had his breakfast. She tells me that he has. She tells me that she was going to complain about early morning noise in the kitchen but since she has this black stallion, she doesn't hold much against him. She fills me in about their early morning conversation around the table.

In her words, 'He's lived in a cave for a significant period and has seen the worst form of hunger. He's eaten leaves and stolen poor squirrels' cache. He's once tried to milk the red deer. He's stolen pheasant and partridge eggs and to my horror, he's killed crows and roasted them during one frozen winter. Poor man has stolen food from every forest creature. No wonder hunger resides in his belly.'

To me, it all feels unbelievable. I'm confused about what I hear but I'm also incredibly sad to know that he'd had such a tough time. I assure Morag, 'He's in good hands...We'll not let him starve in any way. He was a visitor...a stranger but now my employee and a house mate...God knows what else he's going to become to all of us.'

I think Oona should come home soon. I have an inherent need to talk to her all the time. She's a remarkable person; sometime I wonder what I've done in my life to deserve such an amazing woman.

As I pour a final cup of my morning coffee, Séamus enters with Rowan and that reminds me about the kennel. He pulls the chair, takes his seat as Rowan is enjoying a tight hug in his bare strong arms.

He looks at me mischievously saying, 'Someone had the company of pixies last night...the parcels in the dispatch basket tell me.'

We both laugh and I tell him how happy I was. He asks me if I had more orders. I shake my head in negation.

We go down stairs to the workshop and there's another surprise. He's been busy at night. I remember leaving around midnight and there was no sign anywhere that he was awake. I guess, he likes working in privacy.

I'm really pleased with him. I tell him to check the website for orders if he has time while I go to the post office.

Now, I'm sitting in my car with the bundle of parcels, to be dispatched, at the back of my seat and I'm delivering this news to Oona. I tell her that she's in for a huge shock on her arrival; a change has come to the house and to our new business which we'd been wishing for; however, it isn't the change but the pace of change which has baffled me. I hope nothing evil comes out of this incredible venture.

Séamus's proposal for renovating the garage has impressed Oona, which now seems inevitable since my last visit to the workshop this morning. It's heaving with production. Oona's happy but cautious the way our little business is taking off. She tells me to let Séamus stay in the guest room until she comes back and she'd decide his room. The guest room hasn't been busy. It belonged to aunt Jean who now comes over very occasionally.

I drive down the hill; serpent-like, wet, black winding road feels incredibly smooth under the wheels. It's a beautiful day even though it's overcast. Everything around me seems vibrant and rejuvenated. I think it might be my enormous excitement rubbing off on them.

I'm in the post office now. It's unusually busy. My parcels are on their way now and I'm coming back with new supply of postage material.

Back in the workshop, Séamus is packing fresh orders. I guess nearly ten are already in the basket and he has a list in his hand.

I can't contain my joy, my eyes are welled up. I know another run to the post office is required this afternoon. I'm blessed to do these post office runs for Séamus. He gives me the list as he says, 'I think your car is going to fall in love with this downhill road, making to and fro journeys.'

He leaves me with the postage and packing to carry on his work. As I paste the addresses on the parcels, I think I need to speak to Séamus today about the renovation of the old garage. We can't not have it now. I'm not sure if he wants to do it by himself or I need to hire a few more workers. We need to decide on these things soon.

Now I have a bag of parcels more than twice the size I took in the morning to the post office. As I'm leaving, Séamus arrives at the door as well with his binocular around his neck and Rowan in his arms. I guess he's going to the Loch and I'm alright about it. I offer him to join me as I'm going down the hill as well. We have a quick chat on the way. I tell him that garage renovation is now vital and I ask him if he'd join me for purchasing the material. The deal is done. Tomorrow is the purchase day. He is away to the Loch and I to the post office.

***

I'VE JUST UPDATED THE WEBSITE; there're only eight parcels to pack tonight. As soon as I do this, I've to go to bed. I need to get up early. My young business is growing faster than my expectation and my aging bones need to keep pace with it.

I turn the light off and leave the hand written first wage envelope for Séamus. It simply says, 'Thank you very much Séamus.' God knows well, it comes from the depth of my heart, and I mean every word of it.

Lying in my bed, I'm thinking that Oona has no idea how much change this stranger has brought with him. It seems heaven has opened its closed windows to shine upon us. Séamus has freshened up the house and energised me. He's a wind of change in this tiny world of mine.

I've already phoned the electrician. He'd check the connections in the garage to make sure that everything is safe and secure. Séamus said that if someone else looks after the windows then it would free him to be in the workshop, which is crucial now. Supply and demand needs to be balanced. He's already stocked the popular items. He's amazing, always ahead in this game so far.

For the last few nights every night, the last thought in my head before I sleep is Séamus. He's not only filled my workshop with his artistic genius but my mind is replete with the questions about the enigmatic statements, he drops every now and then, and the information he shares sparsely.

I'm sure there's a lot about him, which we don't know, but there's definitely something that is unusual about him. I suspect, it's going to shock us but I may be wrong. He could just be an organised man with dogged determination.

I've got to know all about him, one way or the other.

***

I'M SITTING HERE QUIET, pleased with everything which has happened. It's amazing that one person can become central to your life overnight.

My business has taken off, my bank account is gradually swelling which gives me assurance that I don't have to sell the house and move to the lowlands. I'm capable of looking after this stone giant, which had sucked most of the money of my grandparents. But they loved it and so do I. My love for this house is like no other love.

It makes me wonder why the human heart sometimes is stuck loving things that mostly bring misery and hurt. I guess sages would say that the pull of love is stronger than the tug of hurt.

Anyway, this is where the stone house is now with plenty of fire and wood to keep the cold at bay.

I've just brought a huge pile of our wooden item stock to the fully furnished new garage. It's remarkable that the caravan is holding everything else, which was in the building before.

As I open the door of the garage, I can't stop smiling at its transformation from hoarding junk to holding completed items, and shouldering my wood business. Its walls are painted but bare at the moment except for bunches of heather, Séamus has displayed. Oona will take care of it. Séamus and I have to do the business side. I guess Oona can forget about her little business, whatever she's thought about, for a little while. Her help is valuable to the business.

Morag's been doing the post office runs as well. She's away for some days and we've already finished the frozen cooked food that she had left for us. My desire for food is increasing with everything growing around me. Séamus has a good appetite and an incredibly fine taste too.

I guess, it is either him or me, going to be chef tonight.

***

I JUST HAVE A PHONE CALL from aunt Jean that she's coming for a flying visit. She's on holiday with her granddaughters in the Highlands. She knows that Oona is in Iceland and she reminds me not to worry about a meal. They're going to bring takeaway with them. I'm relieved that I don't have to worry about organising a meal.

I look around; the house is fine only the dining table and the kitchen need some attention. One can tell that the women of this house are away. It's amazing that the woman's interest and presence in the house shouts loud. This house is aunt Jean's childhood home and she still likes to come every now and then. Oona and I try to make her really comfortable.

I've just seen a car on the road coming towards the house.

My aunt has arrived. I receive her at the entrance. She's looking radiant for her age. I've not seen Katrina and Sarah in a long time. They're striking young women. They are both in the university now.

Aunt is curious about the transformation of my garage. I don't tell her anything yet but lead her to it. She reads the sign on the door out loud, 'Beloved Wood' and turning towards me asks,

'What are you up to Hamish?'

I tell her about my business and she's impressed that we eventually decided to go for it. She also thinks that there's so much land around the estate that could be used in some ways to generate money. She knows that it's an expensive thing for me to do, nevertheless she drops her idea.

Inside the house, her favourite spot is the conservatory. She tells me that she used to call the conservatory 'god's seat' because it gives you a wide view of the surroundings, and I think she's right.

I put the food on the table, and call the three chatting women. They're standing on the stairway, talking about aunt Jean's portrait. It's beautiful. Looking at her now, one can't recognise that it's the same woman. Don't take me wrong. She's still a gorgeous and graceful woman but I'm amazed how time changes everything in its realm.

Eventually, aunt has managed to pluck her granddaughters from the staircase and has planted them on the chairs around the dining table. I need to tell you that aunt Jean is a chat leader around the table. It's fun to have people around. It makes you feel that you still live connected in the land of the living.

Now, the girls are putting the dirty plates in the dishwasher. They've kindly offered to make us coffee. Aunt Jean likes strong coffee just as I do. She knows, I make nice coffee so she asks me to treat her with real McCoy coffee.

As she takes her first sip, she tells her granddaughters,

'Umm, this is the one thing we MacKenzies do best.'

Her granddaughters are laughing hilariously as she tells them,

'Your grandpa, poor man, hasn't managed to learn to make the only hot drink I like...every morning...bless him, he wakes me up to...a cup of coffee...what I call...let's say a cup of 'crow's tears.'

She makes me laugh too; she has a strange way of saying things. Perhaps it runs in the family. She's pleased that I still laugh at her jokes and she reminds me, 'Don't ever forget that I'm your wee joker.'

It's nice to see an elder member of my family. The girls are still giggling. I remember, Morag has made rhubarb crumble that should be enough between all of us.

I come back with the sweet and find aunt Jean has picked up Rowan. I didn't see them coming. Séamus is standing in the door in his fine Chisholm kilt. His hair all around his face and he's looking a real catch.

Aunt Jean hasn't seen him yet.

As she lifts her head up, her eyes fix on his face, the smile has vanished from her face and with a faraway look in her eyes she says,

'You are his grandson, aren't you?'

Séamus looks a bit puzzled as to who this woman is who claims to know his grandfather. He comes forward, shakes hand with her and hesitantly responds, 'Yes madam, I'm named after him, Séamus Chisholm.'

She kisses his hand saying, 'Bless you...how come you're an exact replica of him.'

Holding his hands, she looks at me then winks and carries on with a mischievous smile. She says to Séamus,

'You have a charm just like your granddad...I warn you...stay away from my granddaughters...they are pretty, young and crazy...I bet that they'll fall in love with you.'

He laughs it away saying, 'Pretty they are indeed but I assure you that they're safe.'

Then immediately she changes the subject and asks, 'Is your granddad well?'

He seems uncomfortable as he's being asked about his family, which I guess he doesn't like. Eventually he affirms, 'He passed away many years ago.'

I tell aunt Jean that Séamus is my new employee. Her eyes look sad now but she approves of my new employee saying,

'You could never get a better employee than Séamus Chisholm's grandson...look after him for me. Will you?...It's an order...He'll turn round your business just the way his granddad did with Loch Lochy distillery.'

Aunt Jean winks at both of us and then says to me,

'Make sure he doesn't leave you...his granddad left us.'

I look at Séamus with a huge surprise. It's a real news for me that his granddad had assisted in establishing Loch Lochy. Now I know how he got to taste Lochy whisky.

I tell Séamus that she's my aunt Jean and immediately he steps back startled with bewildered eyes as if I dropped a bomb. I can see his eyes are welled up immediately. He bends and coughs to hide whatever has shocked him about my aunt Jean.

I invite him to the table for coffee, and aunt Jean introduces her granddaughters to him. I notice that something is bothering Séamus. He's sipping his coffee silently without taking part in the conversation. He doesn't look at my aunt at all. His eyes are fixed on the floor as he swirls his drink.

My aunt keeps talking to him.

She touches his hair saying how someone can get the exact set of genes to look like their granddad. He just shakes his head saying, 'Believe me, weird things happen...actually stranger than fiction itself.'

Aunt puts her arm around him now and asks, 'Did your granddad find that necklace he was after...He was desperate to get it then.'

He keeps swirling his drink and simply says, 'Unfortunately not.'

'Ah...well, it's such a shame...but you know what, he had you...a gorgeous boy...so I guess he got over that obsession.'

Séamus is silent, just puts on a fake smile for the spirited lady. He finishes his coffee and leaves quickly saying, Nice to meet you Madam.' Aunt Jean has also noticed his red flushed face and I tell her that he's fallen out with his family so I think he just got upset.

Aunt Jean looks sad now as she says, 'How come his grandson became homeless...Let me talk to him.'

Somehow, I don't want aunt Jean to talk to him. I go after him to see if he's ok.

I find him standing in front of aunt's portrait.

He sniffles, as the tears he tries to hold back are not going down well. He wipes his eyes and face, and tells me firmly; 'Please don't tell her...women have a habit of making things complicated.'

'I'm not going to say anything to her but it troubles me...you're upset over something.'

He goes downstairs; without looking back he assures me, 'I'll be fine.'

A train of thoughts and a string of questions are building up in my mind about Séamus, but the time is not right now. I need to get back to my guests.

Aunt Jean and her daughters are ready to leave. She tells me that she's going back to Devon. It's actually nice to see her. I don't see her often and the distance between us doesn't help either. We live in opposite sides of the country.

I see them off, waving as their car descends fast like the speedy youth behind the wheel.

My excitement about meeting my aunt Jean is slightly dampened by the misty eyes of the one who steers my new business.

I've things to ask Séamus but I know he's upset over something and I don't want to be the one who causes more misery. My curiosity can wait. For the time being if he doesn't want to share aspects of his life, it should be fine with me. He's a free man and he keeps secrets from me; this I know for sure.

***

I'M AMAZED THAT MY PARCEL bag is growing enormously day by day. I could have never done this on my own. Séamus is a blessing to me and saviour to this house. I recall what aunt Jean said, 'Don't let him go' and I think only a fool would let him go.

I've started to feel that other than carving wood in my workshop, he has carved a special corner for himself in my heart as well. He's going to stay around.

It's pleasant outside; the sky has put a display of dusk colours in the west.

I'm speaking to Oona. She's pleased that I'd had a family visit. She's close to her family and sometimes she feels for me that I don't have family around. Before I get off the phone, knowing the ingredients in my fridge, she tells me her simple recipe to stir fry beef strips, and I think that it will work perfectly well tonight for Séamus and me.

There's still lots of cod in the fridge. Oona loves cod; cod is in her blood. She says that they don't waste anything of cod. The parts they don't use, they export to other countries.

I love meat and steak. The cave man has not died in me just as the seaman is alive in Icelanders.

Now, I've set my ingredients out on the work surface and my herbs are chopped. Dill is Icelanders' favourite herb. Our fridge never runs out of it. I guess Dill to Oona is what Thyme is to me.

I've already made my sauce. Potatoes are par boiled. Beef has to be stir fried just before serving so I'm waiting for Séamus. I can delay as I'm not starving at the moment.

I'm reading the book Oona bought me a few weeks ago about Iceland. It's a remarkably beautiful country in the middle of nowhere. I know this is my next holiday destination. It's an interesting country and invigorating people; I have one in my home.

I can see from god's seat that Rowan and Séamus are coming. Rowan is running ahead while Séamus is carrying what seems a small bundle of something. I need to be in the kitchen now.

My table is already set, wood is burning gently and the place is pleasantly warm.

Séamus looks calm and content as he normally is; the sting of whatever pricked him in the afternoon seems to be gone now. He tells me that he's spent time walking on the hills and has collected a bundle of heather which surprises me. He has huge bunches of heather already in the garage.

He's really enjoying the food. I ask him if he cooks and he tells me that he's been cooking for a long time but he doesn't consider himself a good cook. His response is peculiar, 'I'm an opportunist diner...I've been eating whatever is the local produce according to the seasons and age.'

He's dropped another reference to time and I wonder what he's trying to tell me. I wonder if this deliberate mentioning of time is to make me think about something specific or maybe he's just weary of time and its treachery.

He's fond of meat and tells me that the best meat in the world is lamb fed on heather.

I'm pleased that he is relaxed and chatty.

He carries on, 'Scotland has an unbreakable bond with heather. It was everything to people when they didn't have much of anything.'

He's younger than I am, and I wonder how he can speak with such a conviction as if he's lived through those old times, he talks about.

I'm nodding my head, taking in the information, he's sharing with me. He further informs me, 'It has fed domestic and wild animals and served its people well.'

I know that it's an abundantly growing shrub in Scottish hills and moors but I don't know how it has served its people, so he tells me,

'This humble shrub has the strongest bark of any tree or shrub...and has been used inside and outside the house by crofters...heather thatched roofs, heather ropes, cooking and heating fuel and even as insulation against cold.'

I'm a patient soul but my curiosity can't be contained now, and I eventually ask him, 'Have you used heather in any of these ways, you just mentioned.'

He immediately replies, 'Almost all of them.'

I hope, he's not lying to me to prove that he is an eco-friendly guy of glens and bens. I'm still thinking to pose another question, and he tells me that he's going to make me something of the heather he has collected today.

To be honest, my brain is all mince now. It's stuffed with lots of questions and inquiries. He somehow makes me speechless, and I feel strangely intimidated to probe what he talks about with such a conviction.

Tonight, I'd have liked to enjoy a round of whisky by the fire, talk to Séamus about things I'm curious about and to play Cluedo or any other card or board game Séamus would like. Unfortunately, he seems to be keen on leaving. He notices the Cluedo pack and says, 'I love it and actually I've one of the first versions of it...will show you...someday.' He winks stressing the word, 'someday'.

Before we leave the dining hall to pursue our evening chores, interests and activities, I propose a meeting during the week.

Séamus's gone to the garage with his bundle of heather leaving me startled at all the things he has said.

I pour some more Loch Lochy whisky and enjoy it, sadly all by myself; only the crackling wood and glowing flame witness the reverence I have for this drink.

I've packed the parcels for tomorrow, left Séamus's wage on the table, the last thing I do every night before I go to bed.

My mind is too full to fall asleep immediately. It's long before I go to sleep tonight.

***

TO MY IMMENSE SURPRISE, Séamus is already sitting in the conservatory. He's set our coffee table, and the kettle is steaming and roaring in the kitchen.

He's looking fresh like a new spring day even though he's worked late last night. The new items and his finished projects in the workshop testify to his late night toil or perhaps early morning labour...I simply don't know.

I'm becoming very fond of him with every passing day but also very curious to know what he's not told me. As he pours coffee for me, I grab the opportunity to start conversation before he sets the trajectory of our talk.

Taking the first sip of my coffee, I start talking,

'So you are an exact replica of him...I find it a bit uncomfortable that you hid the vital information about Séamus Senior and his association with Loch Lochy Distillery.'

Calmly and gently his response is,

'No...it's not true. I wasn't hiding anything from you...just...sometimes it's best that certain things are left unsaid until the opportunity arises.'

I recall hearing my granddad talking about Séamus Senior and I think I should tell Séamus about it so I continue,

'I know 'Séamus Chisholm Senior was a significantly important man to my granddad; a corner stone in establishing Loch Lochy Distillery...I remember being told that Séamus Senior was like a water spring of a special taste...and when he left, unfortunately that unique flavour left the distillery as well, and they could not produce Whisky of that standard again...also they say that the production of whisky reduced as if life was sucked out of the machinery, and energy drained from every soul working in the distillery...My granddad was a proud man, he couldn't justify producing and selling substandard whisky...so sadly he sold the distillery...but I'm completely unaware of why he left.'

Séamus runs fingers through his long hair, shifts on his chair as if restless and responds to me, 'It's a shame that Loch Lochy was sold...I'm sure Séamus Senior didn't mean to harm the business...but now I've come to help you...I'd like you to own the distillery once again.'

I'm really shocked to hear Séamus say this. I want to tell him that although he's a master craftsman with woodwork, but just like me he has not much insight into how hard and difficult it is to run a distillery. I simply respond to his innocent wish,

'Séamus, firstly, I think it's too grand an ambition at the moment...and secondly, do you know why your granddad left the distillery?'

He immediately says, 'Firstly...nothing is too grand if you have a desire, and a willing and loyal employee. Sometimes only one is more than enough...I'm at your service...and secondly, the reasons for Séamus senior leaving...to be honest I don't think we should be talking about our ancestors who worked together long time ago…It has all been said, listened and done before us.'

He's frustrating me. Honestly, he is like an iron teat: as nothing comes out of it so it's nearly impossible to squeeze information from his mouth. I am trying to be patient with the tone of my voice as I say,

'Well, it's great to know about your loyalty but what can you tell me about that necklace?'

I notice that a sudden sadness has descended on him, and I can't bear to see the feeling in his eyes and misery written all over his face. I almost regret posing this question.

He is silent. After contemplating for a few more moments he says, 'I want to find that necklace…It's been lost to me for far too long…I need your help. It's an heirloom and I should have it.'

'Of course, what belongs to you should be yours,' I assure him.

I wish Séamus said something more about the necklace. We both are silent. Eventually he says, 'I think Jean, I mean aunt Jean would know about it.'

He has surprised me again by calling my aunt by her first name. Now, I'm sure that necklace has some kind of story involving my aunt. I throw another question at him,

'Why did you cry when I saw you standing in front of aunt Jean's portrait?'

He's clearly agitated and doesn't want to respond to it.

He throws a glance at me as if looking through me, 'I don't want to talk about my personal life...so excuse me if I refuse to answer your question.'

He has gracefully shut my mouth but now I'm hungry for information, so I find myself blatantly asking another question,

'What does that necklace look like?'

His hand is raised to his neck; I know that he has a silver chain around his neck. He takes it out to shows me the pendant as well and says,

'This is the replica but I'm after the original necklace...and I guess it's in this area...either in the house or out in the ground.'

As soon as my eyes perceive the image of the pendent, I know it's the same necklace which is around my aunt Jean's neck in the portrait. The pendant is a shiny tiny horse's head. I'm surprised, too many horses I have seen and talked about since Séamus has arrived here. I wonder, what horses to this land and house are. I don't say anything further to Séamus.

As he looks at me, his eyes are full of expectation for knowing about the necklace. But even if I know it tonight, I'm not going to gratify his hunger easily until he satisfies mine.

I think we both would go through a period of frustration. I know that hunger of heart is deeper, painful and unbearable than the hunger of belly.

***

I'M STILL THINKING ABOUT the necklace, the horse pendant, the one outside the distillery, the wooden horse Séamus created for me and the one he's given to Morag. I also recall what he'd said something like...'Too much land and not a horse in sight.' His love for horses is evident.

I'd like to know the significance of this necklace, he is after. However, before that I need to look for it in the house.

I want to ask many things about the distillery and my granddad but Séamus is always in hurry and feels a little unsettled. I hope he'll settle down better once Oona comes back. She is a warm-hearted woman with a welcoming and kind spirit. People say that a woman of the house wins hearts.

A few more days of waiting for my wife. I miss Oona more than ever. I think, I'm falling in love more and more with each passing day. Is this me or do most men go through this...I wonder if she feels the same for me or not. I'll consider myself the luckiest man alive if she feels the same as I do.

To be honest, I've never felt this before what I feel for her now. Not having her around the house is like missing a part of me...and I mean it.

Whenever she leaves for a longer period of time, something of the house and something of me goes with her as well, leaving behind a sort of emptiness which seeps through me. I think I would be lost without her. I'm very much looking forward to share all the news and progress about the business.

I hope, she'd like Séamus as much as I do and his dog too.

***

THIS EVENING I PRESENTED the kennel for Rowan to Séamus with a new dog blanket that arrived today in the post. I am a little late in delivering it but it's better to be late than never. He's over the moon and I know Morag will be pleased too. She's been complaining that she had to remove lots of dog fur from the duvet cover.

Tonight, Séamus cooks us an evening meal. It has been a pleasant day so he has organised a barbecue out in the garden.

He's annoyingly economical. He doesn't waste anything. He serves the little pieces of leftover meat and fat from my plate to Rowan saying to me, 'It's lucky that you weren't born to a peasant family in the middle ages...The world has seen some unimaginable episodes of hunger and thirst.'

I can't decide if he's expressing disapproval or pulling my leg or pouring out information about himself. But I tell you that no one can ignore the references to time in his chat when obviously he wasn't even born in that period.

Whatever he's up to, I'm trying to ignore his economic attitude. However, to appreciate his culinary skills and celebrate the enormous work of the day, mostly, done by Séamus, I treat ourselves with...guess what...Lochy...What else is worthy to be enjoyed in the Highlands.

Only three more bottles are left to relish. I'm glad that I can share this beautiful drink with someone who has a connection with its origin, and I know Séamus is fond of it.

I drop a random question, 'What was Séamus senior like?'

His eyes are telling me that he's crafting an answer. Even though he hasn't spoken a word, somehow I know in my bones that he isn't going to give me a straight answer. He responds,

'You know what...I'm Séamus senior.'

I think out loud, 'What the hell.'

He stops for a moment, looks at me and continues, 'You know I'm a physical replica of him but also I work like him at enormous speed...so what he was...is what I am.'

Once again, he reminds me that he'd help me to re-establish the distillery. I seriously think that it's impossible at the moment and my stern response to him is, 'It's crazy like nuts...It's like growing an oak tree overnight.'

He smirks as he answers back, 'All the oaks start as nuts.'

He is damn right. We both laugh.

I ask him why he wants me to do this and he simply says, 'Because we can do it...You understand the business and I know the waters...of this area...perfect for whisky.'

I'm pleased at least some one recognises the importance of my degree in business which I have no faith will get me employed living in this part of the Highlands.

I tell you that he knows how to motivate, stimulate, and energise me, but deliberately I don't want to agree with him tonight on starting anything new. It seems too good to be true of me thinking to be a distillery owner.

It feels as if he has a strange affinity for Highland water, especially for Loch Lochy. I can't fathom his obsession for this Loch. A part of me believes in him but a part of me is also highly suspicious of his enigmatic conversations. He's something to belong to and I hope he remains important to me. At this point, I wish I had a daughter. He's extremely attractive and not just a pretty face but also a very talented and likeable person.

Anyway, for the moment, we have a fledgling business and we better look after it. He's the force behind it. I can never do the work as fast as he can and I'm already thinking what if he leaves us. It will bring the business down. I need to make sure that he stays here. That seems a bit greedy that I want him to be around for my business but to be honest I like him as well. He's a great company. He's a good man, has a place in my heart, and it doesn't really matter how mysterious he is.

I ask him about his age and he wants me to guess. I guess that he's 25 years old. He likes my guess but still doesn't confirm his exact age, only says, 'Some people at a mature age haven't lived at all but some at the age of 25 might have lived for a thousand years.'

I agree with him adding, 'Life is all about experience...it isn't the number of years one has lived but the experiences one has.'

He likes philosophical chat and so do I. I must be getting old that I care for the deeper and bigger questions of life. I often find myself thinking about our planet earth, its resilience, fragility, and I wonder what's going to happen to it. We haven't been kind to it in spite of the fact that it has cradled the human race offering its lands, mountains, waters, forests and what not. We haven't got a planet other than this one, and the human race is stupid and selfish beyond measure.

People say life starts at forty and I wish it were true. I ask him, 'What's the best thing next to life?'

He immediately says, 'Death.'

To be honest, I'm startled. His words send a chill down my spine. This isn't a sort of response that you'd expect from a young man. I know a little about him. He fell out with his family. It must be terrible to make the decision to leave one's blood relation.

I look at him in bewilderment. My ears don't believe what I just heard. This one word has sent chills of enormous magnitude down my spine.

He continues, 'Too much of anything makes it ordinary...smaller and shorter is sweeter and pleasant...the longer you live, the more it adds to the stacks of your loss.'

In spite of all my doubts, I uphold this one truth about him that he never fails to surprise me. He's like an old owl, full of insight dropping prudent words. I can't not say this to him, 'Either you have read too much or have lived life too much...which one is true.'

He laughs and says, 'To astonish you more...both.'

Perhaps, he's pulling my leg now. Our conversation carries on; taking different twists and turns as Lochy travels from the bottle through our glasses to our insides warming up every sense.

He asks me, 'What do you find irresistible in life?'

His question has forced me down the memory lane. Certain things have bewitched me for a while and I say,

'I guess, it's changed over a period of my life. But now it has to be watching dusk approaching with its alluring colours and charming light as the sun sets; starry nights and full moon fill me with awe and thrill.'

He's smiling. I'm sure, he's picked up the string of contrast between our irresistibilities. I guess that for him it is horses. He's been carving a little horse head on each item, he creates. He's wearing one around his neck. I wonder why he has a dog rather than a horse. Then immediately it makes sense to me; when life is rough and tough, a dog is a good friend.

He's clever and knows that I have a question for him too. So he says, 'To answer your unasked question which I see in your eyes...water and the love of women are to me...what these heavenly bodies are to you...irresistible.'

In one word, his answer is surprising and in two, unexpectedly surprising.

I think Lochy is beginning to have its magical impact on me and I guess he's getting under the same influence. I think out loud, 'Very earthly taste...water is essential and I guess no man is immune to the second one.'

Here is a man in my company...a young man talking about the things of this earth and I, talking about the sun, moon and stars. I feel old, very old, just like the heavenly bodies I admire. I contemplate on his response and say to him, 'Well, the choices of your irresistibility are plenty and in abundance.'

He's sitting relaxed; his legs stretched out and his head on the back of his chair. He's staring somewhere far, without looking towards me he says, 'Not really...I've starved for both of them for ages.'

I think out loud, 'What?'

Honestly, I find it hard to believe what this handsome man is telling me so I say, 'Don't tell me that you didn't have a girl friend?' and he simply responds, 'Oh no...I've had almost thousands...none of them stick around.'

I find this man very dramatic and an extremist in his opinions. At one point, he's starved but at the same time he has thousands. I find myself responding, 'I doubt it...convince me.'

He smiles and answers my second unasked question completely ignoring the comment I just made, 'There's too much water around...calling me... but I just hadn't been able to return to it but I'd love to...wait...wait...I have to do.'

Immediately and unexpectedly, he gets up and begins to tidy up the area saying that he will take care of the kitchen too. As he leaves, he shouts back, 'The sun has gone down but the other heavenly bodies will not be too long.' I smile at his comment. It's a pleasant evening. I've enjoyed my day, business has been good, the meal was delicious, company superb and chats peculiar. Séamus has dropped so much interesting information about himself that in spite of my lovely drink, I'm still thinking about him. He never seems to get drunk, no matter how much he drinks.

***

I'M AWAKE SINCE THE EARLY hours of the morning. I suspect that even during my sleep, my mind and heart never slept knowing that Oona is coming home. The feeling reminds me of our younger days; the emotions I had of joy and excitement every time when she came to see me. I must say that she's a 'present' to me, nothing less than the heavenly bodies I admire so much. I wish I'd wings to fly to the airport. I'm looking forward to having her with me.

I must admit that days have flown by swiftly. It doesn't feel that Oona has been away for a month. I guess it's been busy. I'm sure the extent of the business taking off, and the garage transformation is going to be a shock for Oona.

To tell you the truth, it feels impossible that only a month ago our business took its first baby steps. In this period, I've created only a few pieces and my biggest projects have been the driftwood table and Rowan's kennel. It feels pathetic but, to be honest, now I feel a lesser wood worker in comparison to Séamus. He'd been very creative, which has kept me busy up and down the road to the post office.

Séamus has become a business partner without any paper signing ceremonies. A mutual trust has developed between us regarding work, and division of labour has naturally occurred. He's taken on the role of a master crafter, leaving me to look after other aspects of our business. I'm not complaining about it. It just seems a perfect arrangement.

I'm in the workshop to pick up the delivery bag which I got ready last night but I see that there's another huge bag which Séamus has prepared this morning. I'm amazed that orders for 'Beloved Wood' are growing like wild mushroom. I'm so pleased that Oona's going to be around. I've to tell her a lot; business, future of the business, and the mysteries. She's my rock and I depend heavily on her.

There is something else on the table. A note says, 'wonders of heather.' It's a heather woven doormat and two beautiful heather woven baskets. I'm impressed how professionally perfect those baskets are. They're rustic and seem to be from another world. I'm speechless. If I was a child, I'd have believed that elves had woven them while I was asleep. There's something quite magical about them and about him; their maker.

As I leave, I see Morag has put flowers around the house. It looks beautiful and welcoming. I think what would be this world if there's no Oona. Women change your world, I believe this. I've seen mine changing.

I care for this house. I was worried about looking after this huge and impressive stone building, but now my 'Beloved Wood' is thriving and helping to keep the stones fed and warm. Cold stones are good for no body. Without wood they would kill you surviving themselves for ages and weathering well themselves. It's the humble wood, the heat and the light that it exudes, makes them worth living in.

Wood is burning in my hearth but the wood in my workshop is generating money; the fuel for running our lives.

***

I'M TOTALLY EXHAUSTED. It has been a long day. I travelled but not as much as Oona did. I'm a 'delicate man' as she often teases me.

Oona is home and I'm more than pleased. She's still chatting with Morag. I need a wee nap before I go to the post office for the last run of the day. It's a small bundle to carry so it should be quick.

I can tell you that Oona is over the moon to see so many things changed. She's thrilled with the transformation of garage. She already knows what she wants this transformed garage to be. She's hinted that it can be a display room rather than just storing items.

The moment she saw the horse inside the house, she was astounded.

Just like me, she's finding it difficult to believe that all this work has been done in a month and mainly by one man. I mentioned to her on the phone how fast Séamus works but I don't think, it registered properly in her mind.

She seems to be a little suspicious about the whole production. She's right to think that he must have had some help to accomplish all this.

She has fallen in love with the heather woven baskets and has already claimed one of them for her wool and needles. She's a crazy knitter. Whenever she comes back from Iceland, she brings loads of Icelandic wool and I mean loads. She can't sit still. Her hands play with wool and needles most of her waking moments. She tells me that Icelandic women have elfin hands. They create things of beauty and joy. I agree with her. She knits beautifully and sings songs of 'Lopi' wool.

Oona is incredibly industrious and artistic. The funny thing is that she hardly paints at all here. She paints a lot when she goes to Iceland. She's been painting, I can tell you as she's brought back many canvases with her. Everything is packed so I've not seen anything yet of her magic with colour and canvas.

Now my eyes are heavy. I can still hear Morag and Oona chatting and laughing. It's amazingly pleasant, there's something magical about woman's laughter, and my house sparkles as she giggles. My world would collapse if she's not there.

It's beautiful to love but it is also frightening when your life begins to take shape around the existence of one person.

***

IT'S AN EVENING TO BE TREASURED; everyone is happy, chatty, relaxed and it begins to feel like a family of four. I don't know if others feel like this or not but in the last one month life has grown a bit wider and taller for me.

Morag and Oona has served us a lovely meal. I've not felt so satisfied and happy for a long time.

I'm still thinking of Oona's reaction when Séamus came in to shake hands with her. She immediately wiped her face as if she felt a faint water spray.

I've already told Oona that Séamus has been homeless for a while. I'm pleased that we both are happy to provide him with accommodation as he offers his services to us.

After the formal introduction, during the conversation Oona says, 'That horse is wonderful. It looks like a task done by elfin hands...perfect...out of this world.'

Séamus smiles and looks immensely pleased with the compliment. He raises his eyes as he takes a bite of bread, 'Only a lady from the land of elves and trolls could make this comment.'

Oona laughs and says, 'True...absolutely true'.

Oona also admires the skill and effort he put in making the heather baskets and he says, 'Well, I can be a good 'heather Johnny.'

I don't know if Oona understood the term. She's just nodded. I'm sure, she'll ask me later. But I know about Johnnies. It's an old profession; selling things door to door. So in frivolous mood, I ask if he has worked as a heather Johnny.

His response is, 'Oh, heather and me...go a long way back...just like every Scot.'

I think that it doesn't. I'm older than he is and I've had nothing to do with heather. Again, his answer isn't straight but enigmatic.

I'm not a big part of the conversation tonight. It's the three of them. I'm enjoying, absorbing and observing.

I think Morag likes him. How can she not as he responds to her shy glances well. I remember what he said the other day about woman's love. He throws a lovely smile and a magical glance every now and then at her. I hope something beautiful develops between them. They'll make a perfect couple. This match making mentality makes me feel old.

It's a shame that Morag will be leaving to go to college soon but I'm sure we'll keep in touch and hopefully she'll be back with us again, and Séamus isn't going anywhere any soon.

Morag is serving dessert and I'm helping her. I'm clearing the table and listening to their conversation too.

Séamus asks Oona, 'So what are you by trade?'

I just want to tease Oona so I respond to Séamus' question immediately, 'Oh, I know...she is elf by trade.'

He laughs saying, 'Be careful...you might be right.'

She tells him, 'I was trained as an artist but I have other hobbies such as wood and glass engraving...I have a thing for wool so obviously... knitting etc.'

Séamus runs his hands through his hair and I know Oona has noticed a big scar just like I have. She's bold and points toward his cheek and ear asking what happened. He rolls his eyes, taps his fingers tips on the table and his response is, 'It's a dirk cut...I mean a big knife...a small sword.'

The champion of words seems to be struggling to find a suitable word. I wonder where he has lived. It's not the age of swords and samurai.

He immediately adds, 'I've some bad memories...but let's not talk about my bad, dark days.'

Now Morag takes the lead in changing the subject and asks Oona about Icelandic folklore.

Oona replies, 'We've trolls and elves...We call them huldufólk...like every Icelandic child, once I truly believed in elves...with pointy shoes and pointy hats...People still put little elfin houses in their gardens and we don't remove big boulders from the roads.'

I don't believe in such stories. I'm trained in physical science and my mind is not ready to accept this. To me, the explanation and rational for doing these acts is providing for wild life in gardens or not to disturb the wild life under the stones or on hills or whatever the people of Iceland call Elvin chapels or houses.

Oona continues, 'Iceland is a rugged landscape traversed by black craggy mountains, glaciers, boiling ground spitting hot waters...you can't live in this landscape and not believe in a force greater than you...We are not uneducated peasants...look around and you'll understand why the tradition of folklore is so strong here.'

I breathe out and put my arms around Oona saying, 'Wow, Iceland spoke.'

She smiles at me and tries to escape from my arm, 'Stop teasing me. You need to go there and see for yourself...your rugged Scotland, God's own country, looks like nothing rugged beside the raw and brutal beauty of Iceland...yours is a soft pastel water colour painting by comparison.'

The artist within Oona has given us a brief synopsis of her homeland. She speaks with so much passion. I'm so proud of her. She is my encyclopaedia to Iceland.

She directly asks Séamus's opinion about beings like huldufólk. He looks genuinely serious as he airs his opinion, 'There are things which exist but people don't want to try to understand them...Human inability or unwillingness to comprehend their existence doesn't mean that they are not there.'

I think, I'm outnumbered here. I'm just an ordinary human. All three of them around the table have some sort of acceptance of the possibility of something else in our world.

Morag is curious; one can see it in her eyes. Her elbows are jammed on the table like two elegant pillars, wine glass is clasped in her hands and her head is tilted towards Oona. Her curiosity in the subject is evident as she asks another question, 'Oona, have you known anybody who had an encounter with huldufólk?'

Oona pours wine for herself and offers it around the table. She takes off her warm Icelandic cardigan and puts her hair up with a clasp. I guess the house is pleasantly warm enough for her. She comes from a colder country but always complains of being cold here. She misses the natural hot geysers, which heat their houses directly.

She sets her arms gracefully flat on the table and responds to Morag, 'I haven't personally but...my mother told me that as a kid she saw an elf playing piano in their house...People have vivid stories about their encounters. But I still have to meet one for myself.'

Séamus is listening intently and I know a question is brewing inside him. It feels as if I'm attending a seminar on huldufólk. Yes, I was right. Séamus has a question, 'Is there any indication about relationships between humans and huldufólk?'

Oona immediately responds, 'I've heard many romantic stories of huldufólk and ordinary folks...but it was always the humans who moved to their world...never heard of huldufólk leaving their world for humans...'

Now I jump into the conversation, 'I think...I know such a romantic story.'

Oona looks surprised. They all look at me. They know that I don't believe in such stories. So they are curious to what I tell them. I continue 'I know an elf who left Iceland for Scotland.'

They all laugh and Oona yawns and makes that cute face which she always does when embarrassed, and says, 'Oh you...stop it...listen guys you need to come with me to Iceland and experience its magic for yourself.'

I think Oona is feeling sleepy now. She had a long day and a tall bottle of wine as well. I think everyone has enjoyed this evening, the meal and unusual chat about huldufólk in a home in Scottish Highlands.

I'm going to help Morag to clear the kitchen.

Oona leaves the table as she says to Séamus, 'I'll organise your room in the next few days...I hope you're comfortable. We're fine with you staying in that room but don't let aunt Jean ever know that you stayed there...She's still possessive of her old room.'

He smiles with a forlorn look and I find it hard to decipher what's written behind that smile and glance.

***

I CAN'T BELIEVE THAT 'Beloved Wood' our business is six months old and it is pretty successful. Our bank account is healthy; the house is fuller and warmer. Séamus is as industrious and mysterious as ever. Sometimes, he disappears for a day or two. I never know where he goes. I guess, he goes to visit Morag but I'm not sure. He's private so I don't want to be intruder in his life.

To my surprise, Oona tells me that since she's come back from Iceland, the house feels filled with something magical.

I've been feeling this all along but I always thought it's been my sheer excitement which I can't contain within myself, pours out and makes everything charming.

She told me last night that she always found it hard to look after her indoor plants. Now they're thriving and even the pots in those corners of the house where plant always died have amazed her. She also finds that house isn't as cold as it always was.

I actually agree with her. I've always lived with chronic fatigue but now my arms and legs don't know anything like this. I run up and down the stairs and many trips to the post office.

One thing which has made Oona really convinced of this change, is her knitting speed. She thinks that she's faster and more energetic. She has never felt her needles and fingers moving so fast. She feels that she's been finishing her knitting projects faster and faster.

Not only that, she has also been working on her wood engraving project and feels the same. She's excited, telling me that her new glass engraving kit has just arrived last night.

I think that the atmosphere is conducive and stimulating as the three of us are working hard, and this motivates us to work more and produce more; but Oona always has another explanation. I'm not denying the possibility of that but I have my alternative explanation of this surge of energy which Oona and I both are aware of.

To me, it is three like-minded people with industrious and driven nature are causing this surge.

***

IT ISN'T A SUNNY DAY but still nice to lie here on the sofa and rest. Oona is using her glass engraving kit. She showed me earlier the jars and bottles she's going to engrave on.

Today we're also going to have another meeting. Oona has a plan of her own little business. She's been helping us with 'Beloved Wood': packing, posting, purchasing etc. Now she thinks that she needs to bring her own dream to the realm of reality.

I hear footsteps, and I know Séamus has arrived for the meeting. I'm not sleeping. My eyes are closed and from the corner of my half-open eye, I see. He lifts his hat as he says hi to Oona. He's surprised at what he sees and says, 'I see you have got Robert Burns' stylus.' Oona has no idea what he is talking about.

Every Scot knows who Robert Burns is but I've never heard of his stylus. Oona asks, 'Who is he?'

A smile graces his eyes and mouth as he takes his seat nearby. Putting his hat on the table and running his fingers through his wavy hair he responds, 'I guess Hamish hasn't transformed you into a true Scot yet...Robert Burns is a Scottish poet and he was given a diamond pointed stylus by his patron, an Earl...and the poet used it to scribe verse and his signature on windowpanes and glasses.'

Oona really finds it interesting and responds, 'Well, windowpane and glass engraving I can handle but...verse...is far from my potential.'

My mind can't keep up with the surprises, I get every time Séamus says something.

I serve coffee before we start our brief meeting.

Oona tells us that she wants to convert the old ford van into a mobile home and shop. She's been working on her wood engraving, her paintings and knitting, and she thinks she can start a mobile shop.

I didn't see this coming from Oona. She doesn't know much about this kind of trade of mechanics and builders. I'm not useful for this kind of work. So I guess, Séamus is the one who we're looking to for an answer.

Oona wants to know if there's enough money to do this. I guess it's a little complicated, we need to know a rough estimate of the expense. I know that it's important for Oona and that was her dream which she hinted at when she was in Iceland.

Séamus says that money shouldn't be a problem as long as it's doable, and offers to help with Oona's project, which is very generous and sweet of him.

Our meeting ends with the decision that Oona has to do some research to find out about everything for this transformation. She's excited and apprehensive at the same time but also believes where there're three people agreeing on something, anything should be possible. We finish our meeting with another round of coffee and kleinur, a perfect mate for coffee, which Oona has made.

I leave Oona and Séamus for my last run to the post office while they both go to survey the old van. I think if this project works, it will be another blessing for both of us, especially for Oona.

As I'm driving down the road, it suddenly occurs to me that I've not done my search as diligently as I should have. I was supposed to tell Séamus about the necklace. I'd promised him that I'd start looking for it. He's asked me three times now about it.

I'm really feeling bad now. He's always there to help us and I keep forgetting what he needs. To be honest, it isn't a deliberate act. It's been so busy recently that I didn't manage to think or do anything other than my beloved wife and 'Beloved Wood.'

These two beloveds, lovingly and pleasantly, fill my days and nights.

**

I'M IN THE MOOD TODAY but I don't know where to start looking for his necklace. He's firmly asked me not to mention the necklace to anyone. So I have to be a bit secretive.

I'm in the basement of the house. Coming here is as if I've stepped in a cold storage unit. I feel the dense cold hangs in the air as I can see my own breath floating like faint plumes of smoke.

I look around and I can't decide where to start. There are huge cupboards, hunting gear, hats and boots, an old table, huge books, an ancient family Bible, a huge iron bound chest, like the one in pirate movies. All of it means nothing to me but suddenly the old Bible catches my attention.

On lifting it up, a few silverfish drop down on the floor. I'm amazed that it doesn't weigh as much as I expected by its enormous size. I open it; the book falls from my hand. There's a huge hole in the centre of the book and a handful of silverfish.

I shiver because I'm cold but also at the fate of this book. As I stare at it, this little Bible eating silverfish has stopped wriggling as if saying to me, 'We didn't let it go waste...'

It hurts to see that these little insects are so resilient that they've survived the frozen winters in this basement. A thought crosses my mind that they've been feeding on the word of God, and my mouth widens in a smile. But deep down in my heart, I'm really upset to see the Bible in this state. I feel sympathy for it, like a soldier for its fallen comrade.

I lift it up, trying to get rid of all the little monsters. I find a cloth and dust it out. I don't read it any more but it has changed the world in so many ways. It needs to be respected. I put it on the top shelf.

I look around. Everything is covered in dust. I can't stop thinking that all these things have had their full life and now lying here crippled and broken. I'm sorry to see that dust is eating them and cold torturing them. They could be put to good use. But I need to concentrate, charity work is for another day. Today is the day of the necklace.

I'm looking around to start somewhere. There are small wooden boxes on the floor. I begin at the right hand side of the row. I'm looking for a jewellery box. I assume it will be in a box. I've opened all the boxes of this row; mostly books, candle stands, china dishes, albums but no necklace.

I've spent a considerable time here with no luck and now I'm shivering like crazy. I need to get out. This shaking bout is a reminder what the cold stone can do to you if not heated.

Now, I'm sitting beside the fireplace in the dining room feeling safe. Fire has driven the cold out of my body and I'm feeling much better now.

I hear Oona humming in the kitchen. I ask her to make me a cup of coffee. She's surprised how I got that cold to shiver. So I tell her that I was in the basement. Of course, I don't tell her the purpose of my visit there. Not yet.

Oona sits beside me hugging me tight and it feels so good, one of my best treasures.

She's very excited as she tells me that she's found a man who has done a van conversion project like hers. He's given her a rough estimate of the money required and also that he's coming to see the van in a few days.

She also enlightens me that she wants everything in the Van to be made of wood, which Séamus has agreed to work on, but the rest of the work like painting the van, putting the new engine in etc. is going to be done by an expert.

I'm pleased that she's independent and pursues her own projects. I tell you, occasionally she drives me crazy. Sometimes she thinks of the impossible.

She shows me the plan. It's not just a mobile shop; it's a little mobile home. She says that she can drive it down to the lowlands, stay in her van, sell her handiwork and explore Scotland. This plan includes me too.

Now she's showing me her finished craftwork.

She's already packed mittens, gloves, scarves and hats in transparent bags. They're tied with beautiful ribbons sitting in a huge basket like Santa's. She's also done new wood engravings. These items are packed as well again in transparent sheets with cute ribbons.

She's one of the most positive people I have ever met. Her mobile van isn't even ready yet and the items for sale are already on display. She's amazing, thinks bigger and plans ahead always. Her heart is of fire and nerves of steel. She warms my heart and strengthens my will too.

The doorbell rings and I know that it must be our huge delivery of wood for Séamus.

***

I USED TO THINK THAT bedtime is for unwinding, resting and being told a story but not anymore; not at least tonight. I have a lot on my mind. I can't sleep and am tossing around. Just before coming to bed, I had a few glasses of wine with Séamus. I asked him how he could do everything so fast. Why does he sleep very little? Why his hands aren't bruised when he works with wood.

As usual, he didn't give me straight answer but just said, 'This is just the way I am.'

But I didn't let it go this time and I kept asking until he couldn't take my interrogation. He's surprised me with a strange story.

He told me that once, he was caught in a storm somewhere on the hills. He managed to reach a nearby village and took shelter by the churchyard. In the morning, an old man, probably a monk, saw him and offered him something to eat. He took him to a warm place and fed him well. In return, Séamus wanted to help him. The old man was putting a roof on the old barn. Séamus stayed and before the evening fell, the roof was in place. The old man blessed him saying,

"you're kinder than most humans...May you never get weary in body and mind, may your shoes and clothes never wear out and may the place and people be blessed wherever you land."

I'm surprised that he believes that the prayer of the old monk has been his strength since then. To be honest, it feels as if he's told me a fairy tale from Middle Ages. To me it is unbelievable.

He's told me that he rarely buys clothes and shoes. They don't get old. His kitchen supplies don't run out. Honestly, I was jumpy and a little apprehensive sitting next to him. What he told me feels like miracles that I've known from my long gone religious beliefs.

I want to know more about him but this revelation by Séamus makes sense in the context of our life since he arrived at our door. Now I know the surge of energy, a flow of production and a rush of activity in this house, which Oona talked about, and I've experienced too, is perhaps the blessing that Séamus carries around with him. I find it hard to believe though.

I feel uncomfortable because this is something that doesn't tally with my scientific thinking. However, I feel lucky that he's landed here at the right time when we needed him.

I don't know if I'm supposed to believe his story, sit relaxed and enjoy the hard work of my employee with special powers or lose sleep over it. Whatever I should do, this account of his story is going to stay with me forever.

To be honest, after this revelation, I don't want to lose him. He's like the goose who lays the golden eggs. But believe me I'm not entirely selfish.

Séamus is a very gentle soul, good company, an intelligent and industrious employee but above all, I like him. He has a place in my heart. I don't know what to call him; my friend or my son or what, but all I know is that he's important to me and it reminds me that I've to talk to aunt Jean about the necklace, Séamus is looking for. I've been visiting our basement off and on but I haven't had any luck or success so far.

I look at Oona. She's sleeping peacefully and snoring beautifully. She's my strength. She believes in me when I'm nothing but a doubting Thomas. Hugging her, I wish that she rubs off her sleep over me tonight too.

***

IT'S WILD OUT TODAY: the sun has vanished, clouds have taken over the sky and the wind is howling like a beast. It's terrifying to witness the raw power of nature. Today, it's best to remain indoors.

Oona isn't happy. Her van's new engine won't be installed today as the mechanic has called off because of the weather. She's already done some work. All the old entrails of the van have been removed; either sold or trashed. Paint has given a new look to its body and hopefully a fresh start.

I've called off my round trip to the post office as well. Séamus, the workaholic, is in the workshop.

Rowan is running around the house following Oona wherever she goes. It's incredible that Oona has found a corner in her heart for this adorable beast. I often find him sitting at her feet near the fireplace when she knits and occasionally he gets cuddles as well. She has always been against me having a pet. I'm not complaining just stating the fact that life changes in unexpected ways by unexpected beings.

Right now, Oona is in the porch. I've recently made her a new shoe bench and she's cleaning the area for it. I better go and help her.

The indoor shoe rule is very strong in this house. Oona doesn't like outdoor shoes taken in. I think it's something Icelandic in her. We've many extra pairs for the visitors. I'm putting the shoes on the new shoe bench and I notice that Séamus has a pair of long boots and walking shoes. They've got some dirt on them but they look new.

I hold them and whisper to myself, 'miracle boots.' I decide to clean his shoes. I feel my heart overwhelmed to do something little for him. I really feel for him that he'd had a tough time and it's sad that he has fallen out with his family. It must have been very hard for him. We're glad that he's around and he's brought me a fortune just by being in this house. I haven't told anything, about his bestowed magical powers, to Oona yet.

Rain is still coming down in buckets.

I just got off the phone. I hoped that aunt Jean would enlighten me about the necklace and Séamus senior. But all she said, 'Séamus senior is all in my past now but the necklace you should look in the basement or attic. It must be in the house. Once I took it off, I didn't know where it was.'

I think I should resume my search in the basement; it isn't finished yet and then I'd look in the attic just above aunt Jean's room.

***

OONA HAS ORGANISED a weekend trip for all of us. We're going to Edinburgh for Morag's 21st birthday. We couldn't make it on her birthday so it's a belated celebration with us. She's special to us; a part of our little family, at least, for me.

In addition to this, it's a very special trip because we're travelling in Oona's mobile shop. It's an unbelievable transformation of a Ford van, exhibiting incredible craftsmanship.

It's spacious beyond imagination and the interior woodwork is just brilliant. There's a bed for two, which can be converted into seats for travel, good storage, small kitchen, microwave, kettle, essential utensils, and even a tiny fridge. I never knew one could create so much space in this tiny Van.

Oh man, I'm speechless.

There are tables on both sides of the doors to display Oona's craft. The tables are retractable like cat's claws. The only thing that the dweller has to constantly look for is the bushes and running water. You understand what I mean. Yes, there is no toilet facility in it.

We're already in the restaurant waiting for Séamus to arrive. Oona's baked a cake and we handed it over to the restaurant staff for later.

Morag looks happy to see us. She's impressed with Oona's mobile shop and they've already planned that for Christmas they're going to tour around Scotland's big cities to sell Oona's craft and Morag's hot drinks.

I'm amazed how quickly the decisions are made. I need a lot of time to munch and crunch everything before I swallow it. I look at them and consider myself a fortunate man that I'm surrounded by a few but absolutely amazing people.

I can see Séamus has walked into the restaurant and is now speaking at the reception.

I rush to get him. He's a dashing man in his kilt. He hugs Oona and then Morag. He's handed over a tiny gift bag to Morag.

I can see Morag blushes as she speaks to him. He's fine, relaxed, pretending to be unaware about his beautiful self. He flirts with his eyes, smiling lips and chats. She clearly likes him and I think he's fully aware of his charms just like his granddad, as aunt Jean suggested.

We've ordered our meal.

Morag's tiny gift bag has fallen on the floor. The cause of its fall is the huge book-like menu. Séamus hands it over to her saying, 'Don't lose it.'

She's embarrassed as she opens it. In a plastic bag, there is a pearl bracelet. She's pleasantly surprised. I can tell you she wasn't expecting this. As Oona puts the bracelet around Morag's wrist, she says, 'It's gorgeous...what kind of pearls are these if you don't mind?'

He immediately says, 'These are Scottish fresh water natural pearls...actually they are from the river Spey.'

I know nothing about the pearls but I tell you even though they aren't graduated, their various colours and sizes just make them look stunning. My knowledge about pearls is meagre. I only know that the natural pearls are expensive and it's a whole string of natural pearls wrapped round Morag's wrist.

Our meal has arrived. While we are eating, our conversation is still revolving around pearls. Oona says, 'I knew about salt water pearls of Far East but I've never heard of Scottish natural pearls.'

Chewing his steak, Séamus quickly replies, 'Oh Yes, there's been pearl fishing in Scotland for centuries...we do have a famous natural pearl from the river Tay called 'Abernethy pearl'. It's arguably one of the most perfect freshwater pearl ever found in the entire world.'

I want to hide myself now. I feel as if I know nothing about Scotland. Séamus really surprises me, shocks me or leaves me speechless whenever he opens his mouth.

I wonder if there are gaps in my education. I know nothing about the heather trade, about Robert Burn's stylus and now about Scottish Pearls. Where have I studied? Surely, I was educated in a school not behind a fireplace. How come Séamus knows so much about Scotland?

I feel as if I'm a pseudo-Scot in his company. Anyway, pseudo-Scot isn't without a brain. One thing that I know for sure is that selling fresh water pearls is a wild life crime now. So how come Séamus has managed this big string of pearls.

I don't know if the girls are suspicious of him or not but I'm worried if he's involved with some dark business of the endangered species of fresh water mussels. I have to ask him but not tonight and not in front of Morag. These pearls are her birthday present, a precious one, and she should enjoy it to its fullest.

The waitress has brought our hot drinks and the cake has arrived too. I'm sitting on this chair but my mind isn't with the three people sitting around the table. I can't concentrate on the conversation going around the table.

My mind is full of Séamus. Who is he? Where does he come from? Why is he with us? What does he want? He's been brilliant with our business. He's honest but I know nothing about him except that he's not on good terms with his family. Sometimes he disappears for a day or two but I don't know where he goes.

I begin to think there is a dark side to this young man. Natural pearls are expensive. He has even claimed that the pearls are from the river Spey. I'm compelled to think that he's involved with pearl fishing which is a wild life crime. If that's the case then he's a thief.

He's homeless. I pay him well but not so well that he can afford natural pearls. Why can I not afford a string of pearls for my wife? I wonder if he's made up the story, which he told me some time ago about the old monk, the storm and blessing he got from him.

I think my thoughts and feelings have coloured my perception badly just now. Séamus seems to be a well-dressed, cocky man from a movie. He doesn't appear as a genuine man. He seems to be a made up character who is behaving in certain manner because his role requires him to be like this.

The three of them are laughing. I don't know what they are talking about anymore. I need to leave the table now or I'll spit out some horrible words.

I see the restaurant bar. I better go and get whisky. At least I know my dram, even if all else fails.

***

OTHER THAN CURIOSITY building up in my head, all has been well around our estate house for some time now.

I've shown details of our revenue to Oona, the other day. The swollen account has blown her mind away. It feels impossible to achieve this with such a small team of workers like ours.

Oona is a huge devotee of Séamus's talent and work ethics. I'm not a lesser admirer of Séamus but only when he doesn't annoy me with his encyclopaedic knowledge about Scotland, and when he doesn't fill my mind with suspicion and doubts about him. Just like Oona, he drives me crazy sometimes; Oona with her impossible dreams and projects, and Séamus with his impossible, suspicious and outlandish stories.

I still want to interrogate him about things and I mean a lot of things. I'm a patient person and I can let things brew for some time until I can contain them no longer. To me, thoughts are just like whisky held in a tightly closed oak barrel, releasing an angel's share every now and then.

But I have to share a real dram of my thoughts with Séamus.

***

OONA IS OVER THE MOON. Recently, she's been driving her mobile shop every now and then down to the lowlands. She tells me that she's selling her crafts faster than she thought. Some days have been bad when she didn't get much sold but she blames the old enemy, the Scottish weather. I tease her that it's easy to blame the other. I'm glad that she understands my crooked sense of humour. I don't have a sense of humour to share with many people but she laughs at my wee jokes and comments, and that pleases me. That's all that matters to me; to see her smile.

The weather is changing fast. Winter is at our doorsteps. As I'm driving down the road, I see all the golden, brown and auburn colours of rural Scotland and I can't but feel awe, and my heart is filled with overwhelming love for this beautiful country.

I've always lived here so I don't know the feeling of missing my homeland. I know Oona gets home sick. Once she said to me, 'What do you do if you want to hug your country.' And I think is there such a thing as hugs for your country but then I question myself what will be equivalent of hugging a huge piece of land with its mountains, forests, lands and rivers which you love.

I find patriotism a strange and powerful feeling. The object of its fixation is huge, a country. This day, time and moment, I know that I love this place. Canadians might be proud of their autumnal colours, and Icelanders about their wild and brutal nature but ours is God's own country, after all made on the eighth day of His creating bout. A smile spreads across my face and it warms my heart to think that I live in a stunning place.

I've posted my packages and the lady at the counter is having a wee chat with me about my trips to the post office and I am talking about 'Beloved Wood.'

As I leave, I get a call from aunt Jean. She wants to talk. So I tell her that I'd call her back soon. I steer my car towards Letterfinlay lodge house on the banks of Loch Lochy. I need a wee break to talk and I can spend some time at the bank of Loch Lochy.

Oona is not home. She's gone for a huge purchase in preparation of her Christmas projects. I'm pleased Séamus has accompanied her. It's wild out today. Surprisingly, she's recently told me that she's scared of strong winds. Does that not sound crazy to you? Yes, to me, it does.

I mean...she comes from a wind battered country and you know what...I think my woman in all her beauty, charm and talent can still prove herself a little bonkers. But in spite of all my loopy thoughts and opinions, I love her to bits.

I've ordered my black coffee. I call aunt Jean. Her first question is if I've found the necklace. My immediate response is in negation.

She asks me what Séamus says.

I inform her that I'd a chat with him the other day. I apologised for not being able to find it yet, and all he had said was 'As long as you're looking for it earnestly I'm fine.' He says that it's an heirloom and that he wants it back. He doesn't seem to be in hurry though.

Aunt Jean sighs. She tells me that she really feels for this lad. She's asked me a million times to look after him.

She seems to be in a relaxed mood today so I gather my courage to pose the question. 'Aunt Jean, what do you know about Séamus Senior?

She heaves a louder sigh this time,

'Oh come on...you're not interrogating me on his granddad now.'

She stops for a moment and then continues,

'Well, the truth is I knew him at a very close and personal level...things didn't work out for us...I don't want to talk about it...ask something else, let's not dwell on ancient history.'

But I think, I shouldn't let the opportunity pass by. She's invited me to ask, so I do,

'Where did the necklace come from?'

She's chiding me gently, I can hear that in her voice but I can sense that she wants to help as well. Her response is,

'I don't actually know...It was in my mum's jewellery and I started wearing it...I don't know how he knew that I had that necklace. Dad said that it was up to me to sell it...you know Séamus...I mean Séamus Senior wanted to buy it...I'm not sure but I think that he fell out with dad over this necklace and then left...I took the necklace off and nobody talked about it afterwards...Dad tried to look for Séamus but he just vanished...for many years, he searched for him.'

Aunt Jean is off the phone now. It was an interesting call. I haven't found the necklace yet but I know a lot more about it now. This brief family history and insight into what might have happened has spurred me to go back and look for the necklace. It's become important to me too now. It was in my family's jewels, my grandmother owned it before Séamus senior knew about it. So it's mine.

Now I feel the ownership of it. I think, it's going to be a challenge to prove who the rightful owner of this necklace is.

Let's see how this unfolds itself.

***

THE FIRST SNOW DUST of the winter has descended on the bens and glens. The forecast for heavy snow is issued. It's lovely to watch the snowfall while sitting inside the house, having a warm drink and wrapped in comfortable clothing. I've just returned from the post office. It's bitterly cold out there. It seeps through your body and seems to break your bones with pain. I'm glad to be in the pleasantly warm house where freezing wind can't chase me. They are locked out.

The funny thing about winds is that sometimes, they feel animated as if somehow possessed by some kind of a being. It's amazing how winds behave differently leaving diverse impact.

Believe me, there's nothing more tantalising than a flirting and tender spring breeze caressing you all over but I tell you that Oona is also right to think that it's terrifying being chased by winds; howling and prowling like a mad beast taking away everything that comes in their way.

I don't know what has possessed the wind today. I can see it's trying to bend the trees and bushes against their natural inclination. It makes them groan, shout and cry as their twigs break and the trunks refuse to bend the way the wind wants them to bend. I don't think that wind likes this irritability. It's trying hard to uproot them. I can't see the winner of this contest yet. Both seem to be determined.

As I take my boots off, Rowan appears from nowhere running between my feet. A tinsel is wrapped around his legs which I guess he's trying to get rid of.

To me, tinsel is a herald of Christmas. I know Oona wants the house to be decked out on the first day of December. I like her eagerness; she makes my house beautiful. Christmas decorations and lights create something magical. For one month of the year, I'm happy to live in the world of magical tales of elves and Santa.

'Wow', is the first expression that falls from my mouth, as I enter the sitting room.

The fireplace is already looking exquisite: wood is burning, four stockings are hanging by it, and cards on the mantel piece are placed. A string of Christmas lights is blinking around the fireplace. It looks like a scene from a Christmas card.

I take the empty log basket from Oona's hand and I'm going to get it filled. On the other side of the fireplace a Christmas tree is standing, bare at the moment, surrounded by boxes. Boxes are labelled as 'Scottish' and 'Iceland'. I know she has certain things from Iceland like her advent wreath with candles, Christmas elves, and Santa's sledge, and straw Christmas decoration, an origami style huge star for the window and nativity scene. One box is for outdoor decoration.

As I load the log basket beside the fireplace, Oona asks me to put her huge star in the window and also the Christmas lights and garlands on the banister.

She's also telling me that she's changed her mind and she's going to Scandinavian countries with Morag taking her mobile shop to a Christmas market. It's a surprise for me. Sometimes, her mind changes as the Scottish weather does. But at her heart, she is ice and fire, both strong and determined to do what she wants. I'm glad to have her around me.

I leave for my postage and packaging job; this is the first Christmas season for 'Beloved Wood' and I must say it's pretty good so far.

Séamus has been doing some bespoke Christmas orders and other regular items of decoration and furniture. He'd been busy as hell. I don't complain or compete with him anymore. He's a blessing, if there is such a thing, and I'm an ordinary human being.

The bundle of packaging is growing and I'm not finished yet. For the first time, I think that the customer should give me a break.

Oona has come downstairs now; strands of tinsel are stuck on her jumper and hair. I tease her, 'Mobile Christmas tree.'

She is tired but of course not admitting that. She says that she wants me to put up her outdoor Christmas decorations.

I think it's insane. It's snowing outside. She's determined to get it ready and says that she'd do it by herself.

Séamus offers help and now out of guilt I feel bad. I say to her, 'Séamus and I are enough. You let us know what to do and get us something nice to drink and eat.'

After all, it's the season for food lovers.

Outside, we've put up a huge reindeer, an elf and holy family, lit. It's started raining heavily now. I don't think it's a good idea to stay out in the cold.

Séamus volunteers to finish the task and I run around like a headless chicken. Eventually a huge string of lights on the bench, just outside the house, and a few metal hanging decorations are in place which make a lovely sound when pushed by the wind.

The outdoor decoration is done as best as we could in this weather. Now both of us need warmth. We run towards the house. Our feet are soaked. I take my socks off by the door but Séamus doesn't. He goes straight in with soaked feet, and I know Oona isn't going to be happy with his dripping feet.

We stretch ourselves in front of the fireplace. The air is laden with the smell of cinnamon and I know Oona has mulled wine for us. As soon as she serves us, she shakes her head; she has noticed dripping feet. She goes back and brings him a pair of fresh socks; of course, they're mine. I look at her and she makes this cute face.

Séamus is talking about the mulled wine, deliberately ignoring the socks that she just handed him. I know what's going through Oona's head. It's interesting to watch her. I bet she's thinking, 'How dare Séamus has dripping feet on my carpet.'

I tell you that she's run out of patience. She moves forward, takes the wine glass from his hand and says, 'Take your socks off and get yourself warmed up.'

She brings him a small towel for drying his feet. I notice his feet; they are damp but look clean, fresh and smooth. I'm ashamed to say that the skin of his heels is more attractive than my hands. In nervousness, I run my hands on both sides of my face. Oona is watching him as well and suddenly his toenails grab our attention.

They are silver and shimmering. They have this iridescence of fish scales or seashell. I'm actually freaked out but Oona is impressed and she says, 'Wow, lovely nails...How did you get them done...I'd like to have mine like yours?'

I think, this man is a freak. Whatever he shows us, raises questions, I wonder what other surprises he's hiding underneath his chic clothes.

I can tell you that he's annoyed at being forced to take his socks off. He's wiping and drying his feet and eventually when he puts his socks on, he says, 'No Oona...You don't want to have toe nails like mine. They stay forever...and everything to do with forever is painful.'

He leaves, taking his mulled wine and saying that he's loads to finish tonight. And I think, pearly string and pearly toes...something for sure is very odd about him. The trouble is, I have to be a bit rude, a bit thick skinned and make him sit down so that I can ask him the many questions which are brewing in my head. As soon as something odd happens, is revealed or is said by him, he just takes his leave. But the good thing about me is, I can wait...so I'm after some rightly ripened time to break open the pumpkin of my doubts, suspicions and questions.

I'm sure Oona and Morag must have their own inquiries as well but we all are private to some extent.

***

OONA HAS WORKED HARD over the last few weeks. I packed her woollen items last night in transparent bags. She's excited. Scandinavia is not new to her but for Morag it is. Séamus has carved a lovely wooden sign 'Beloved Wood', painted in Christmas colours, adorning her mobile shop now.

Before they leave, I serve 'Whip Col', a traditional Shetland Christmas drink. It's an amazing festive drink and an old recipe of my grandmother, she was a Shetlander. Oona loves it and she calls it 'Viking breakfast'. It's indeed a rich drink to beat the cold.

Oona gives small gift packs to me, Morag and Séamus, saying, 'Put them on or Jólaköttur will eat you.' I know what she's talking about but Morag and Séamus don't. I tease Oona, 'Come on my elf...grow up.'

She makes this cute face when she doesn't want to say anything.

Morag opens her little pack. It's Scandinavian patterned ear warmers. She puts them on immediately. Oona makes us sit in the van to put our stuff on. For Séamus and I, it is leg warmers. Mine are green and white. She always chooses green colour for me as I have ginger hair and, apparently, it goes well with my tone. For Séamus, it's red and white. We both put them on. They actually look nice, peeping over the top of our long boots.

Putting my arms around her and looking at her face I say 'Ok, so everyone is safe now...happy.'

Morag asks what it is all about.

Oona is a little embarrassed and her response is, 'Well, don't laugh, it's just a nice tale...Jólaköttur is a Christmas cat. The legend is that it eats people who haven't received any new clothes to wear before Christmas Eve...but it's just fun and a chance to have new things.'

Séamus immediately asks where Oona's new stuff is. She points towards her head shaking her lovely ponytail. She's already wearing her Icelandic headband matching with her beautifully knitted jumper and on top of that, she has wrapped a tartan shawl around her body. I love her eclectic regalia.

Séamus is accompanying them down the road. They've a long drive ahead of them to the south of the country where they'll catch a boat to Europe. I wave at them as they drive away and I turn round to go and get some work done.

The Christmas charms are jingling, the lights blinking, and I can't but think that I might be the ginger but the three of them have much more flavour. They've spiced up my life.

Before I close the door, I look around. The vast land is stretched for miles in front of my eyes. We've plans for it now. Oona and I agreed last night that the next expansion of our business and property is going to be lodges for holidaymakers. This is Oona's idea. She thinks that 'Beloved Wood' isn't sustainable without Séamus and he isn't going to stay with us forever. She thinks that while he's with us we should try to establish something, which we both can run easily when he leaves us. He is young and he will have a life of his own. We have land, so we can make it more useful and profitable for us.

However, there are two things of concern regarding this plan at the moment: the planning permission from the local authority and money. I'm sure that the planning permission was granted previously for expanding the property but I need to recheck with the council. It is a long time since the previous permission was sought.

As far as money is concerned, I'm ready to take a loan and I think we're able to get it. However, Oona also said that we can borrow money from her brother. He has his own business and he can easily lend us money and there will be no interest on it at all.

Every now and then Séamus talks about the Loch Lochy distillery. Oona has interest in the lodges and she can help me to run the business but I'm not sure about distillery at the moment. I'd like to have Loch Lochy restarted but it's bit too ambitious as I previously said to Séamus. It's not right for me to dwell on something that looks impossible to me.

The house is quiet and filled with festive aroma. The golden glowing fire and blinking Christmas lights make it charming. I'm looking at the stockings hanging. I intend to put everyday something little for Oona in it. This is what she wants; to be remembered every day when she is gone.

Rowan has just jumped unto my lap as if saying that he feels lonely. I cuddle him and he licks my nose. I think we both are going to have a wee nap.

***

I'M HOLDING THE FIRST MUG of morning coffee, looking through the kitchen window at the frozen world outside. The fog is still thick across the land as far as I can see; there's no chance of it clearing away any time soon.

Oona told me last night that Europe is freezing as well. Both of them are having a good time. Every time Oona calls me, she's either eating sausages or drinking mulled wine. I'm pleased that she's more than happy with her sales. Morag has made some good money too with her hot drinks but not as good as Oona. I guess comparing hot drinks with craft is like comparing oranges and apples.

Anyway, they're in Sweden at the moment. Oona was asking me to fly over, and join her in celebrating her mobile shop but I'm sorry to disappoint her. There's too much going on here with 'Beloved Wood' and it's too foggy even to go down to the post office today. If the fog doesn't clear then I'm afraid there will be no post office run today. I'm a bit uncomfortable, driving through thick fog descending the hill.

I better go to the basement in search of the necklace.

I've opened the last few boxes in the basement and there are old photo albums which belonged to granddad. With no particular interest, I open one album. In a few pictures, I can recognise Séamus senior. Aunt Jean is right; Séamus is a replica of his granddad. These pictures appear to be from another world: black and white and taken from some distance but I can recognise him in the second row standing just behind granddad. There are loads of them but unfortunately, I don't have time to go through all of them. May be Séamus would like to have a look at them so I put the box on one side.

The last box is just not worth exploring for a necklace. There are loose papers, diaries and journals. They're of no interest at the moment. So that's the end of my systematic search here in the basement. Now I've to move on to the attic.

Before I leave the basement, the old family Bible, which I left on the shelf previously, captivates my attention once more. I pick it up reverently, again dust it out of respect and put beside the fireplace upstairs.

As I go to the kitchen to get something to eat before resuming my search, Séamus comes in and tells me that he's driving down the road to the post office. I'm covered in dust and I feel embarrassed that he's doing my job now. He knows that I'm not comfortable driving through any form of water condensation: snow, sleet, fog or whatever. He just says, 'It doesn't bother me...water could be my element.'

He smiles. As he leaves, I tell him that I've sifted through the basement and that there is no sign of the necklace and his response is, 'Take it easy, I have a patience of thousand years so don't tire yourself...just look earnestly.'

I appreciate Séamus going to the post office. There're two huge bags of customers parcels that he's dispatched.

I am grateful for his help but I can't deny that he's left me puzzled, pondering over the length and strength of his patience; another reference of time.

I just feel uncomfortable about my own thoughts now. I better clear my head of the cobwebs of myths and supernatural things. I don't want to get influenced by prayers of blessing, huldufólk or any other kind of folk lore. I'm a scientist and I should know better than delving into these stories.

I'm in the attic now.

It's musty, not as cold and as full of boxes as the basement is. But there's a chest of drawers here. Aunt Jean told me that she'd cleared the attic a long time ago but there might be some stuff left. It's time to open the drawers one by one. It's pitch dark here. I need some more candles.

There are a few jewellery pieces here and there, among the albums but not the necklace. Another useless day of searching; I haven't found it and I wonder if the sky has eaten it or the earth has swallowed it. It's nowhere to be found in this house. I'm tired and I call it off for today.

I also hear Rowan barking and I guess Séamus is in the kitchen. I have already taken a whole big pack of scallops out for dinner tonight. We are both going to have a man sized portion with chorizo.

Séamus has chopped parsley finely and spring onions along with a huge cut on his left index finger. He's standing, watching his finger bleed. I'm running around to look for my first aid box but Séamus stays calm asking me to take it easy. His finger is bleeding profusely, how can I take it easy. He's already made me feel guilty again today. It was my turn to cook and he was just being helpful.

Now I'm worried that we're in the middle of the Christmas season and many orders are still coming. It's a business nightmare if his finger is injured, unable to handle the tools of his craft.

I'm doing the preparation to bind his finger and you know what he does. He's asking me trivial questions about the black lava salt from Iceland that we use for our meals. I wish he would shut up and let me get on with dressing his finger. Eventually, I've cleaned and tied his finger, hoping he'd be fine.

I ask him to sit down while I finish the rest of dinner cooking. He offers to set the table. It's just the two of us tonight so I suggest that we eat by the fireplace. Séamus has brought my driftwood table by the fire and has set it neatly.

Our seafood is ready. I'm hungry and I guess so is he. Out of guilt, I serve him a portion bigger than mine. I hope, it'll be an enough compensation for tonight. I'm more worried and nervous than him about his index finger. I wish that it heals quickly or at least the pain goes away.

As we eat, I survey his face and his black scar that offers itself to be questioned but today is for the necklace.

Now, as I'm a little more knowledgeable than before about the necklace, and also I feel a sense of ownership, hence I believe I can put forward some complex questions.

He's enjoying his meal. Before I open my mouth, he has already started to speak. He informs me that the black lava salt feels less intense in comparison to white table salt. A thought whispers in my head that I already know about this blooming salt; so it's time for me to probe which I've no or little knowledge of. Completely ignoring his comment that he just made, I ask away,

'How closely did Séamus senior know my family...I mean specifically...aunt Jean?'

He shrugs his shoulders and without looking at me his response is,

'I guess you should pose this question to your dear aunt...Jean.'

He's perhaps right but I'm going to elicit the answer from him tonight so I carry on,

'Well, Séamus...It feels easier to talk to you on this issue rather than probing my old aunt...asking her is a little too direct and too personal, in my opinion.'

He thinks for a while, rubbing his hand against his scarred cheek he says,

'He loved her...and I know for sure...she loved him too.'

He doesn't say more than this.

We both are silent.

He asks me if I've spoken to my aunt Jean and unfortunately, I've to tell him a lie. He's again quiet, and vigorously twirls his Loch Lochy in the glass and smells it deeply as if he wants to take in every single molecule of the drink through his nostrils. But I can't stay silent tonight; my inside is burning with the heat of all that I don't know and I ask him,

'I guess you were told about the necklace...tell me...how did Séamus senior know that the necklace was here?'

He's irritated. He doesn't like questioning but he is a gentle soul so puts up with me. He tells me,

'Séamus senior could sense whenever the necklace was worn...He could tell where it was, most of the time.'

I breathe out heavily as I find it creepy what he's just told me about his granddad. It seems that he's led a secret mysterious life living under the wing of my granddad. I have more to ask but a bit of me thinks that it's unfair to probe him for what his granddad knew but the other half of me says that this is your chance to know. So I go with the latter and I ask him,

'Why did Séamus senior leave?'

He looks at me as if saying shut up but now he's turned his head away from me. He's cuddling Rowan and he says with a kind of sting in his voice,

'We really shouldn't be discussing the details of their personal lives...but briefly, your aunt jean said that she'd get the silversmith to crush the necklace and the pendant too...He begged her not to do that...and so afterwards I think he left.'

His response tells me that there's a lot more to this story, which he owes me. But that's for another day. I just feel that I need to ask one more question before I stop my search for tonight.

I offer him more Loch Lochy. That's the last dram from this bottle, and now I'm left with only two more bottles from my granddad's distillery. Hesitantly, I ask him, 'What's the significance of that necklace to you now?'

His response is in a cold manner,

'As I said previously...it's an heirloom.'

I feel that I've not asked a right question. So I clear my throat to continue,

'What exactly would you do with that necklace once it is found?'

I have a feeling that Séamus isn't going to answer me. But after shifting multiple times on his chair, running his hand through his hair and cuddling Rowan he eventually decides to respond to the question that he clearly hates,

'I actually live for it...this is how much the necklace means to me...and what would I do with it...that's a matter for after it's found and...is in my hand...You get it for me, and I promise to tell you.'

As I wring my hands not knowing what to say. I find myself thinking that it's quite a definitive answer, and even if I have another question, it's not going to fall from my tongue tonight.

Séamus looks at the clock. He offers to help in the kitchen. He is generally quiet but just odd chat about the weather and work...then we call it night.

I'm tired. The work in the cold basement and attic has been hard going. My legs and arms are a bit stiff but my mind is also tired of brooding over Séamus. My doggedness to find out necklace annoys me but also I want to own it.

I battle with myself. Why can I not just accept that the necklace is his whenever I find it. It should be handed over to him. But at this time and moment, there is a split within me; there is a 'good me' and a 'bad me'.

The 'good me' says that people don't want to share their family histories and it's his heirloom. He should get it. But the 'bad me' says that it was in my family before his granddad knew about the necklace, and in addition to the ownership of necklace, the 'bad me' wants to know answers for all the questions brewing within me.

I guess denial of information doesn't go well with me, which is not fair to Séamus because then he comes under the hammer of my questioning, and it makes him leave every single time.

He's homeless, away from his family so I must be kind to him. He had been our rescuer. For the business and house, we owe him. I'm not going to resume my search until after the New Year. It's time that I get to relax, let him breathe as well and not put him under scrutiny. I don't want to grill him but it's just the nature of the subject and him, not being straightforward in answering my question, winds me up.

***

DURING THE LAST ONE week, I've made many phone calls and it's clear that an inspection is due immediately after New Year regarding permission for our log cabin project. I also have to do a lot of other paper work, related to this new business venture.

I'm waiting for Séamus sitting in the conservatory. Fresh snow has fallen over night but the sky is clear now. Everything is white as far as my eyes capture the sight. Sun is shining and snow is glistening. The sky is so blue and the reflection of light from the white sheet of snow so intense that that my eyes hurt to look at it.

We have a meeting today, mid-day. Nothing urgent but I just want to share the news and progress about log cabins with Séamus.

He's just walked in like a mouse today, not even a tiny sound. My eyes are locked on his feet unintentionally and I'm curious why he has silver shimmering toenails.

He knows that I'm watching him but I just comment about his socks. He actually has a fine taste in socks. He wears socks nice and bright at his toes and heels, and I think that if his monk's prayer story is true then he needs to buy posh socks once and they can last his lifetime. But I don't believe this. I need to do a proper observation to establish my opinion about the wear and tear of his clothing. The scientist within me some times put me into a lot of trouble: raising questions, critiquing and eventually barring me to go with the flow.

As I share our plan, Séamus is pleased and willing to help us with the log cabins but at the same time, again he talks about reviving Loch Lochy Distillery.

I tell him that the log cabins are something on which Oona and I both agree. She doesn't have an attachment to the distillery so I don't blame her for not showing any enthusiasm for getting my heritage back and I 'm not ready to take it on my own. In addition, there is money that always runs short, doesn't matter how much one has. It's such a volatile commodity. We need something, which we both are happy and comfortable with, and something that is sustainable for both of us.

Séamus doesn't say anything but I can tell, he's disappointed. I understand that he wants to bring back something, which was the pride of my granddad; and also his granddad was associated with it. It's very sweet of him to think about it. But it's best, sometime, to disappoint someone for the sake of the common good for all involved.

Today is the last day of the postal run for our packages. We are closed from today until New Year. Séamus reminds me that we've to reorder wood. He has brought a list with him, which needs to be reordered. I guess something else is on his mind. He's thinking as he bites his lips.

To my surprise, he asks if he can buy the remaining wood as we are closed for Christmas so the wood isn't needed for at least two weeks. I say to him that he doesn't need to buy it. He can just use it but he's determined that he needs to pay for the wood, he would use. So that's fine with me. I guess he has a plan to surprise us.

We both wrap up warm and go out. I want to show Séamus our plan for the lodges. I tell him that we want to have 10 lodges and a cafe where meals can be served as well.

I've been searching and contacting people and have communicated with some companies for quotes. A manager is coming to see us after the holidays. Nothing is finalised yet, but I've started making inquiries.

Séamus says that he would do the furniture for log cabins. But I think it will be a huge project to be done for 10 cabins. He reminds me that we're aiming to get the cabins ready by summer so there are six months. I guess, he has a point but I'm still sceptical about the timing and the enormity of the project.

I've seen him working at a fast pace but the projects he works on at the moment are not that huge like doing dining tables and other things.

I'm sure the lodge project will take many twists and turns before getting finalised once Oona is involved.

She'll be home tomorrow and we'll have plenty of discussions. I'm looking forward to spending time with her. It's been a busy time since we started our business and Oona started her mobile shop.

To tell you the truth, it's good to be busy and be sure that everything is fine with us. I can't tell you how relieved I am that we don't have to sell our house. It's secure, warm and makes us all happy.

One thing, which upsets me when I look at Séamus is that during the last months, I've succeeded in almost everything we started except that I've failed in finding Séamus's necklace, which somehow bothers me.

The one who is vital to this business still hasn't achieved what his heart's desire is. In spite of my own interest in the necklace now, I feel for him. He has recently told me that he lives to find this necklace.

**

OONA HAS COME HOME. She's fast asleep, snoring and oozing heat, locked in my gentle embrace.

It's extremely quiet inside and outside the house. No owl hooting, no wind howling or rustling. Apparently, it's the longest and perhaps the darkest night of the year; not a single star in sight. But tonight I don't care about celestial stars. My world is bright; my star is with me, and my world revolves around her.

Oona has brought loads of travel success stories but also a surge of activity. I'm part of everything she's doing especially at this time of the year. I actually celebrate Christmas for her. She's passionate about keeping the tradition of her childhood celebrations. I find her passion quite contagious. I myself, somehow, during the ride of this life have lost the meaning of it. It's become just a fairy tale for me.

Oona often says that the scientist within me has taken over my thought process and has left me with no room for things, which don't fit in the framework of scientific thinking. She often labels me as a reductionist and empiricist, and calls for the need of a paradigm shift.

Since Séamus has arrived at our doorsteps, the framework of my scientific thinking has been challenged all the time. He's been doing and saying things, intentionally or unintentionally, which have made me curious, especially the references of time that lace his comments and conversations.

The concept of time has always fascinated me for a long time now. I wonder if time is material or immaterial. Is it an entity or non-entity? Is it under the control of celestial bodies shining upon us determining our days and nights or is it something that resides deep within us. Is it a resource in the universe? Can it be destroyed? Can it be created? Is there an end of time or is it going to outlast everything.

I also wonder how it feels to be eternal where nothing seems to last. You hear that the sun will be no more in millions of years. We also know that our moon is drifting away from our planet gradually, and eventually earth will lose its only moon. I wonder if planet earth will survive to experience the loss of its moon.

My train of thought has suddenly come to a halt as I hear Rowan barking. I wonder what the little beast is doing at this ungodly hour of the darkest night. I wonder if Séamus is up or there is a thief in the house.

Séamus has said to me previously that he and his dog are as harmless as bamboo eating pandas. He might be harmless but neither he nor I am stupid like a bamboo-eating panda. He's aware that I know he's up to something.

I hear a faint sound of footsteps, and I have an uncanny urge in my bones to get out of my bed. I release Oona from my embrace, and tiptoe on the cold wooden floor, creaking under the weight of my body.

I stand in my bedroom door in my cold dressing gown.

As my eyes are trying to adjust to the darkness, I hear whispers near the stairs. I'm scared now. My heart is pounding in my rib cage, and my body is getting tense obviously getting me ready for fight or flight.

I think what if someone has broken into the house; what if they're armed. I grab a curtain metal rod, the nearest hard object, and begin to tip toe towards the stairs.

The invader is standing. I can see the outline of his body. I wish I don't have to throw this metal rod at the invader. I really hope that they go away silently taking what they want and leave us without any harm.

The invader is constantly whispering. I can only see one shadow. I don't know how many there are. I'm holding a humble rod to defend myself in case my presence becomes evident to them.

Suddenly, Rowan comes up barking around the invader. Now I see that he's whispering to one of the portraits along the stairs. His whispers are hardly audible and he goes on and on.

I'm shivering but the Sherlock Holmes within me has just woken up and wants to stay on this task of observation now. I wrap my robe tightly around my body and sit on the floor. As soon as I sit down, he decides to leave and descends down but only to come back, and whispers again, this time a little louder.

My jaw drops as I hear him say, 'You're the only one in a thousand years, I happen to come across face to face in this old age...I wish I'd not seen you...it hurts that you didn't recognise me at all.'

I can't tell who he's speaking to; my grandfather, grandmother, my father or aunt Jean.

Again, he intends to go and descends turning around once more as if he doesn't want to leave. He continues, 'Yes, your granddaughters are beauties but in my eyes...they've not surpassed yours...you're still the most beautiful woman I have ever met.'

It feels as if I forgot to breathe hearing this revealing monologue. The sense of intimacy and informal way of his speech has astonished me tremendously.

I feel a sudden chill running through my spine. A thought crosses my mind. People say that a ghost's presence is manifested by a sudden drop of temperature. I've never believed in such manifestations but I might be witnessing one just now. The iron rod just dropped from my hand and I run to my bed like a cold iguana rushing to the hot rocks. I have brought a kind of earthquake on our bed with my shivering and trembling, and have woken Oona up.

Turning the bedside light on, she looks at me; touches my cold forehead and says, 'What's wrong...You're white as a sheet. It feels as if you've seen a ghost.'

I pull myself deep in the folds of our heavy winter duvet and my voice is muffled as I respond, 'You might be right Oona...I might have seen one.'

She asks me to tell her what happened.

To be honest I'm not sure if it was Séamus or a lurking ghost of Séamus senior. My senses for the first time seem to be endorsing the bizarre physical phenomenon I've encountered. I'm more puzzled by the whispers I heard from the being on the stairs. The content of his speech refers to aunt Jean who Séamus met some months ago but the intimacy and the manner of his speech hints as if he was the ghost of Séamus senior, who now I know was in love with aunt Jean.

I don't know who we're dealing with and who I've allowed to come, work and stay in our house.

Oona gives me water, wipes my forehead and wraps me in her embrace saying, 'The goddess of sleep is never too far away to be invoked.'

I don't wish for sleep. All I desire is that all these magical beings are banished at this point from my house.

***

I'M AWAKE SINCE EARLY in the morning. I think a part of me stayed up even when I was asleep.

Last night, I've lied deliberately to Oona saying that I had a bad dream. I can't reveal what I heard and saw until I know for myself what it was.

I'm up now, in the kitchen with a cup of coffee in my hand thinking that the best place for me is to be in my workshop in front of the fireplace to ward off the chills of winter and the chills of fear.

I can't find comfort here today even though our workshop is a charming, cosy and comforting place. The heat has put a glow on my face as I've been sitting in front of the fire. I grab an old photo album, which I put in my drawer just a few days ago.

I'm looking at my old family pictures from the time when I wasn't even born. Séamus senior is in many of the photos, and I can't ignore the uncanny resemblance between the grandson and granddad. Now, I'm looking at the picture of my dad, aunt jean and Séamus senior. They're standing beside a damaged dyke holding hands. From the attire, it feels a summer time. I just lift the picture closer to my eye when the door opens and in comes Séamus.

He's surprised to see me there, 'Well, the longest night of the year didn't allure either you or me to sleep a bit longer.'

He pulls his chair near the fireplace.

I guess, he realises that I'm not in the mood to speak as I haven't responded to him and not even looked at him. We're both silent.

I'm staring at the leaping flames, without looking towards him. Eventually, I open my mouth, 'You asked for your freedom of choice and you were granted...I also asked for one thing...openness...and you've been keeping secrets from me.'

He stretches himself on the easy chair and responds, 'I haven't said much...because the time isn't right...but I don't intend to keep secrets.'

I don't know what he intends. I say to him, 'Keep one secret of mine as well...I haven't told Oona about it...I've seen something last night and I'm not sure who I saw...I guess it was a ghost of Séamus senior talking to aunt Jean's portrait.'

He sighs loud and deep.

His head is at rest against the chair as he replies, 'I'll keep yours and you keep mine...It was me last night on the stairs in front of the portrait...not a ghost...there is no ghost of him...it's me and only me.'

'So who are you then,' words just fell from my mouth as I turn towards him.

'I'm Séamus...the one who was on the stairs...the one who worked with your granddad...the one who left the distillery...and the one who loved...Jean...your aunt.'

I'm dumbfounded as if struck by lightning. I pull my robe closer to me protecting myself. I want to look at him but just the thought of it gives me goose bumps.

I don't know how to deal with this revelation. How can he be the one in all these times...in the past and in the now as well.

The glow the fire gave me is gone from my face; my energy is seeping through every pore of my body, and my faculties are all confused. It feels as if I'm dreaming. I'm listening to something impossible. I nearly fall from my chair as I ask him again, 'For heaven's sake...tell me...who are you?'

He sees the state of my being drenched in sweat and says to me, 'I know...it's a shock to your belief system...your scientific way of thinking wouldn't support it...but it actually is true...you don't need to be scared of me...I am a...water spirit.'

As soon I hear this I'm on the floor.

He comes forward to help me but I pull myself away from him.

He realises that I'm scared stiff. He sits far away from me while his words continue to shock me, 'I'm a shape shifter...How come you couldn't guess it...Don't you see the horses...They're everywhere...I'm a water horse...a kelpie.'

Now, I doubt the state of my mind, I believe I'm hallucinating or dreaming.

Suddenly, there are flashbacks from my childhood.

I can remember the stories of kelpies told by my grandmother. I can't accept that the shape shifters or kelpies are actually some kind of a real beings. I thought they were fictional...figment of one's imagination.

'See, Hamish...You don't need to be frightened of me...consider me your friend...I'm not going to shape shift into a horse and gallop around. There was a time when I could shape shift into a human or a kelpie...but I can't any more,' saying this he leaves the workshop to get his breakfast.

As soon as he leaves, I take advantage of this short window of his absence and I run out of the room: sprinting on the stairs, not stopping anywhere until I hit the door of my bedroom. I rush for my bed and hide myself in my duvet trying to catch my breath.

Oona is in the shower. She peeps through the door after hearing the bang on the door and commotion caused by my running feet. She sees me in the bed and goes back.

I'm still in a state of shock.

How dreadful it is to find out that the monsters of your grandmother's stories actually are real. I feel devastated psychologically, spiritually, physically and what not. All frontiers of my life are badly shaken.

Now I wish I hadn't pushed him to tell me who he is.

I'm trying to force all these thoughts, words and events out from my mind. I need some respite but I can't find it. My mind is full of thoughts about the magical beings and there is no room to think rationally. I keep thinking about our conversation about elves, the wanderer and huldufólk the other day. I'm terrified at the thought what if Oona is an Icelandic elf and Morag some kind of another magical being.

Oona pulls the duvet gently from my face and I shriek as I am looking at her, terrified, trying to hide from her. She says, 'You had a terrible night, love...bad dreams...sleep for a bit...catch up with your sleep...I need to go down and prepare.'

We're having a pre-Christmas gathering tonight as Morag has to go tomorrow morning to her family for Christmas. Oona is going to have a busy day that is why she's up early as well and gone down.

It's nearly mid-morning. Oona calls me saying that Séamus has asked twice about me and wants to talk. I don't want to talk to a shape shifter at the moment.

Oona forces me out of the bed and into the shower.

Now, I'm in my dressing gown, sitting at the edge of bed and Oona comes saying that she's serving coffee and wants me to be downstairs.

I come out of my room wishing that Séamus is not there. But he's sitting around the table.

I'm delaying my entrance.

Oona calls me, 'Your coffee will be Icelandic water by the time you arrive here.'

I walk in, not a word to anyone.

Oona ruffles my hair, and tells Séamus that I had some bad dreams last night which kept me up.

Séamus suspects that Oona is aware of last night's event. He takes his coffee and leaves saying, 'Oona...you need to believe me...sometimes the real events are far worse than your nightmares...I'll see you downstairs...Hamish.'

Previously, I wanted to talk and he used to avoid me; today he wants to chat and I don't want to be around him at all.

Oona gently forces me to go, 'You must spend time with him to discuss the lodges...He was telling me all sorts of things that he can do...Remember, he's young and one of these days, he'll leave...Let's take an advantage of the help he offers.'

I respond annoyed, 'I don't think he's going anywhere any time soon,' and I'm thinking in my head, 'Don't be fooled...he's an old soul...older than all of us...and is in no rush to go anywhere.'

I still feel incredibly shocked about his revelation of himself. He has also affected my thinking about my own wife and Morag or everyone around me. They could be anyone of these magical beings fooling me around. He's shaken my trust in him, in my rational faculties, and generally about my belief and all that is scientific.

My mood, attitude and behaviour has changed at many frontiers of life but especially towards Séamus.

I'm stone cold and I can't think rationally except for imagining all sorts of beings.

***

I'M FULLY AWARE of the fact that I can't avoid Séamus. I've to speak to him; stakes are high and I have a hunger within me to know his full story.

As I enter the workshop, I hang a sign on the door, 'Do not disturb.' I don't want Oona or Morag to know this mystery of Séamus at this moment.

I also have brought the old family Bible, the one with the huge hole in it, with me. Some silver fish crawl out of it as I set it on my table against the wall to support it. As a child when I was scared, my own little Bible used to be my safety. It had its constant presence underneath my pillow. Today, I need comfort and assurance as the unbelievable is happening around me. If a man can make me believe that he is a kelpie, then this book can be my anchor too.

Séamus looks busy carving wood. I pull my chair and the bottle of Loch Lochy. I don't care what time it is. I need it. I pour it in two glasses saying, 'This all explains your obsessive love for horses.'

Taking his whisky glass from my hand, a smile graces his face and he says, 'Oh God...not really...I actually hate horses.'

He carries on explaining that horses were scared of him. When he shape shifted, horses would gallop away from him. So he wasn't comfortable around them neither were they around him.

I don't know what to say or ask anymore. He continues,

'Hamish, listen...You don't need to be afraid of me...I haven't shape shifted in a long time now...I'm stuck in this body...and even if I do, I promise no harm to you.'

My curiosity kicks in with the whisky hitting my senses. A string of questions is awaiting to come out of my mouth and I start, 'Where are you from then?'

'I told you before...I'm very local...Loch Lochy'

As I recall, his fascination with the Loch makes sense. Lochy is his home.

'How long have you been around?' is my next question?

He keeps shaving wood and says, 'Almost a thousand years.'

It's a bombshell hitting me hard. This all makes sense of all the references of time, he's been dropping in his conversation every now and then. It annoys me that in our plain sight, he's been hiding a truth talking about olden days, olden practices and the story of his broken family etc. I feel cheated. But he says that he hasn't lied, just not revealed himself, as he has to invent himself every now and then in order to fit in.

'Have you ever returned to your waters?' I carry on my questioning.

He stops shaving the wood and replies, 'Yes...regularly...until a tragedy happened and locked my spirit in this human body.'

I don't understand if he can't go back to being a kelpie or if he doesn't want to be kelpie any more. The tone of his voice changes and sadness descend on him. 'Yes, I'd like to go back to my waters but I need my bridle for that.'

I'm not sure what he's referring to. He puts his tool on the side of his table and says, 'The necklace, I'm after...is my bridle...that's why I need it.'

'But that belongs to my ancestors...more precisely, it belongs to aunt Jean.'

'No...It doesn't belong to any human...It's mine and mine alone.'

He looks and sounds frustrated at having this conversation with me.

I can't give him the necklace even if I had it with me today before knowing the story behind it.

I speak, 'How did you know that the necklace was here?'

'It calls me when it isn't hidden under the ground and...If someone puts it on...It attracts me to them...It binds the souls.'

I ask him to tell me the whole story of him ending up at my granddad's estate. Taking deep breath he starts,

'Well...I was in the outer and inner Hebrides for a long time...hopping from one island to another...reinventing myself every now and then...the Isle of Harris, is the place I stayed for the longest...I'd lost any hope of finding my bridle but one winter afternoon...I was woken up by the noise of crashing waves...It was the sound of my waters...Loch Lochy calling me...I hadn't heard this call in a very long time...I knew it was my bridle unearthed somewhere summoning me...I had to leave the Hebrides and I did it in a heartbeat. I wandered around the Highland moors in search of my bridle...The attraction got stronger and stronger...After wandering for many weeks, I was led by the sound of waves to your granddad's door step...As I was walking towards the estate, the sound of crashing waves calmed down indicating that I had arrived at the right place...Your granddad had built the distillery and was hiring people to work...I guess my bridle was unearthed during this construction...well I had to stay here so I asked for any job I could get in his business.'

'So where did you find your...bri...,' I haven't finished my sentence and Oona has just walked in, completely ignoring the sign on the door saying, 'This den isn't just a men's club.'

'Of course it is not...It belongs to huldufólk too...You can come and join,' I reply taking a huge mug of hot chocolate that she's brought for each of us.

We both fall silent, looking awkwardly at each other as if trying to hide something from her. She feels that she's interrupted our business meeting, so she leaves saying, 'It feels as if angels are passing through this workshop.'

I think in my head, 'You have no idea amongst your angels and elves who else has walked into this house.'

She bangs the door behind her, feeling unwelcome; and Séamus continues,

'Well...I didn't find it immediately. It kept calling me until one day when the attraction was so strong...You see it binds the soul of the person to me who wears it...so I discovered Jean had it...I don't think Jean and your father considered me as their equal but they both were very fond of me and so was I...to cut the story short...In spite of my restraints, I couldn't help but fall in love with Jean and she with me...then one day, I felt a very strong pull towards Jean which I couldn't resist...She was out on the moors...I followed her...It was calling me...My bridle was her necklace that day...We spent the whole afternoon on the moors...She showed me her new necklace saying that her mother gave her...I loved her and she loved me too.

'She always had my full attention but not that day...I so much wanted to take the necklace...I could have snatched it from her but the fear of breaking the chain was bigger than the desire of having it in my hand immediately...A broken bridle wouldn't be any good to me...She showed me the horse pendent, you will see there are two ruby red jewels...They are bound to me...and if someone else wears them for a longer period of time they can kill them...so I was worried for her too. I told her that she shouldn't wear that pendant...I actually asked her to exchange that pendent for another pendent which was around my neck...It was a similar pendent...It was safe for her to wear but she didn't listen to me...She promised that she'd change the chain and give that one to me...but she never did...then she came to know the worth of those ruby jewels and thought that I was after the jewels not after her...I was a humble servant but she still wanted to marry me...She broke her own heart...She thought I was greedy for money which was not true...I could have shown her chests full of treasures from bygone days...but women...You know...even a kelpie knows they are complicated...things weren't great between us...tension was always there...She'd stopped wearing it but I knew she had it...Once more I asked her for the chain...and she said that the chain was pulling us apart...and said that she'd get the chain and pendant crushed...It was worse than a nightmare...I begged her not to do this and I actually frightened her by saying that crushing them will bring bad luck to the family...I knew I couldn't stop asking and looking for the necklace and she wasn't willing to give it to me...The only solution for me was to leave...I spent many years away in agony in a cave in Harris till I couldn't hear it summoning me. She hid it somewhere under the ground...so I couldn't hear it again until I came back to you asking for a job and the cycle started again...so I know my bridle is out again somewhere in your estate...Look for it...I'll do anything you say in return for my bridle...until then you'll ask me no more questions.'

From a simple necklace to a bridle, from a human to a kelpie...It was a hell of a story. My whole belief system is in tatters. I'm treading on shaken ground. What is true and what is fiction, is beyond my comprehension now.

I'm in deep thoughts not realising Oona is in the room and Séamus has left. She saw Séamus rushing out of the house and now me sitting in silence; she thinks that we argued and have fallen out with each other. She's concerned about Séamus, business and me.

She doesn't know that all hell has broken loose and I a mere human is scared of everyone around me, even of her...Icelandic elf might she be.

Tonight, I want Séamus to leave us alone, out of our business and everything we do. We'll be fine without him.

***

I'VE SPENT MY AFTERNOON, around the house in the attic. Oona and Morag have made the pre-Christmas evening special for all of us. But my mood is dampened and I can't lift up my soul, enjoy all that has been done and is happening around me.

Séamus has arrived in his dashing kilt with a large and rugged sack on his shoulders, and looks like an outlandish being to me.

I am worried as I see him captivating Morag with all his charms. I wonder how many times he has fooled around innocent women. I remember him saying something about women and irresistibility and mentioning of almost a thousand girlfriends.

He has surprised Oona with a huge set of red deer antlers as her Christmas present. She's over the moon. Red deer, the monarch of the glens, is her favourite animal. She's painted many of them, displayed all around our house.

Morag gets a beautifully restored antique watch, studded with jewels and mother of pearl for its dial. Both women around me are going crazy without knowing whom they're getting these gifts from. I hope these gifts don't vanish. Who knows if they are a product of some kind of magic? I'm very suspicious now.

He gives me a package wrapped in a humble brown paper, 'I don't hate you...I've something for you too...from my so called home.'

My jaw drops and I can't believe it, 'A bottle of Loch Lochy and a pair of Harris Tweed Socks.'

I'm looking at him and he's smiling almost teasing me humanly, 'Except you...no one knows the importance of both these items.'

I know he's a water spirit; Loch Lochy has all the fascination as it was his home, and Harris his earthly abode while banished from the Loch.

Finally, tonight we play cluedo. He's brought his old packet, smelling very musty and showing signs of old age. While Oona is getting drinks and Morag her dessert, in a very mischievous mood he secretly whispers, 'You can keep this...this is one of the first versions.' He shows me the date.

I wish I could share all, which has been revealed to me, to these women as well. But I don't dare tonight. I need to tell Oona at least...soon and very soon or I'll go mad.

Oona has a painting for Séamus. She brings it to him and says, 'From both of us to our loyal employee, and a charming friend.'

I don't know how he's going to react. I know what it is. He tears the packing away, 'Oh, no...a horse.'

He looks at me. I tell Oona that I just came to know today that he doesn't like horses. Oona is distressed that her gift isn't appropriate. She's thinking correctly. We all thought, he loved horses. She says, 'I don't get it...so then...what's this obsession with horses.'

He feels for Oona as she really looks upset. He says,

'When you detest something so much...You become obsessed with it...You don't want to forget for a moment that you hate them so much...so horses and I are not friends...They get scared of me and I of them...but I'll happily display it as a reminder...Don't you worry.'

Trying to forget about the painting, Oona brings me an envelope too, 'To my one and only.'

I tear it open in haste. There are two tickets. We're flying tomorrow morning to see aunt Jean for Christmas. She's expecting us in the late afternoon for Christmas Eve. Oona also informs me that aunt Jean invited Séamus as well, but he's declined and instead he's going to the Isle of Harris.

A secret glance is passed between Séamus and me, and I ask, 'Where are you staying?' He doesn't look me in the eye when he says, 'kelpie cottage.'

'Is this where you go when sometimes you disappear from our radar,' I ask him. He says, 'Not necessarily'; but most of the time he is there, now I know.

Séamus, the old soul and Rowan will be home, our guardian before he leaves for his cottage far away across the waters in Harris.

***

WE'VE HIRED A CAR, and are driving to Devon where aunt jean has invited the family after a long time.

The journey has been pleasant. I love Scotland but it's nice to go away for a short break. Oona has knitted throughout this journey while talking to me on varied subjects. She has no idea what's going through my mind. I don't know what the right time is to reveal this forbidden secret. It's a great distraction and I ask Oona to drive for the rest of the journey.

I'm going to see my cousins and their families after a long time. I thought they might have forgotten about me by this time. Uncle Harrison is an interesting man. I've always liked his company. He's a biochemist and although retired, he keeps doing experiments in their kitchen, with their food, and annoying aunt Jean.

Aunt Jean is genially excited to see us. I'm the only connection from her brother's side. She tells me that she sees her brother and her father in my facial features and mannerism.

Christmas Eve has come and gone. We've enjoyed a nice meal: the refined palate of this family has been well served and everyone is merry and cheery.

Oona has gone star gazing with uncle Harrison and my nieces. It's a beautiful, clear and dark night. The rest are watching something on the TV; aunt Jean and I are all alone in front of the good old fireplace.

I ask aunt Jean, 'Did grandma use to tell you the stories of kelpies?'

Sipping her wine she mutters, 'Oh yea...the one with the beautiful bridle and studded saddle...She used to tell us every time before we would go out for playing...but only to keep us away from the Loch waters.'

'Did you believe those stories?'

'Well...being a child you were scared of these creatures... weren't you?

'Do you think they are real?'

'Oh...come on...I thought you were a scientist...Why would you believe in such garbage.'

'I just wonder...What would you do if you came to know that these were real creatures?' I ask her.

'To be honest...First of all I would laugh at the person who would tell me this...Secondly, I will not go near them;

according to the stories they're vicious...They take their riders down with them into the lochs...They are nasty.'

Saying this, she's disappeared behind one of the doors now.

My mind is in a whirl; laden with the thoughts of beings other than my own kind and I can't shake the thought that they're not the product of one's imagination any more.

I see that aunt has brought two old family albums, which she goes through every Christmas.

That's her private yearly ritual.

Occasionally, she shows a picture or two to me as well. Now she shows me a picture of my parents. I have not known my mother. She passed away after an accident when I was very young and I have no memory of her. My grandparents have raised me with great love and care.

Now, she takes this black and white picture from the album saying, 'Would you not agree that Séamus is an exact replica of his grandfather.'

I take the picture but I don't want to say anything to her and I simply agree with her. She carries on while pushing the picture back in the album, 'It is such a shame that he didn't want to join us for Christmas.'

'He has his own young life to live,' I cover for him but then I ask her, 'What's the story behind this necklace that he's after.'

'Well, I don't know. He was terribly possessive about the necklace, especially the silver chain...It was a very fine chain and I guess...the gems were too precious to him.'

I can still feel the sting in her voice. I understand she was hurt that he valued the jewels and money. Knowing the story, I feel sorry for both of them.

Her ritual is complete now, and she put the albums back wherever she got them from. She comes back with a glass of wine for both of us.

'Were you friends with Séamus senior?' I ask her.

'Oh, well, to start with we were...you know...emotions come and go between young people...'

She smiles and tells me off saying, 'I wasn't always old and haggard...Don't forget once I was young too and had a very romantic heart...so he was a bit...let's say more than my friend...but now you stop asking me any more questions about my old boys.' she laughs.

I tell her that Séamus has shared with me the story and that you had the necklace when he left...I mean Séamus senior.'

'I don't know what he's told you...but when he left...I felt as if I was going mad...and I told our kitchen maid about that necklace...She thought the gems were cursed and could drive me mad...So I took it off and gave it to her to hide it somewhere in the house where I couldn't see it...So I have no idea where it is now.'

She tells me though that I should check in the basement where the old kitchen fireplace was, 'I know the kitchen maid used to hide her valuables under the floor below a loose brick.'

I'm pleased that I got at least some more information to direct my search.

Now aunt Jean sounds tipsy as she says, 'I'm glad your father hasn't left anything behind for you to chase...I feel sorry for this lad that he still has to look for this bloody necklace...Séamus should never have burdened his grandson with his unfinished task...whatever it was.'

I look at her happy face and I think being ignorant over some matters is really a bliss. I have no intention of telling her that the story of her past is still lurking in my house. I just have to deal with it.

I still don't like to think that he's hidden a lot from me but when I think and look at the change he has brought in our lives, my heart goes to him. In spite of being terribly upset over what he's told me, I still want to look after him.

The women in my life, Oona, Morag and aunt Jean, are all incredibly fond of him. I believe that the three of them can take on a battle for him too. It feels as if he's bound to us.

***

LAST NIGHT, I'VE TOLD Oona the forbidden secret about Séamus: the shape shifter. Although he's asked me not to tell it to anyone but I can't keep this burning log within myself or I'll scorch myself with its heat. To be honest, after telling Oona I feel relieved that someone can carry the burden of this mystery with me.

To add to my surprise, Oona doesn't believe a word of it. I'd have thought that her reaction would be a little different from mine as she comes from a land full of stories of huldufólk. A land where they still don't remove the big boulders from the roads, thinking that there's an elfin chapel but she is genuinely as shocked as I am.

We are both fully aware of the miraculous growth of business and all the surge of activity and energy in our house. Oona believes that it's all because of Séamus but paradoxically she isn't ready to accept that he's a kelpie. She tells me that she needs to see it happen in front of her eyes before she believes that he's a kelpie.

She has raised many other questions in addition to his shimmering toenails, the fresh water pearl string, the huge set of antlers and all sorts of other things he's shared with us.

I ask Oona not to ask anything from him yet because I've promised that no one would know about him. Sadly, I've already broken that promise. In my opinion, a humble human like me needs to share things, which are a bother.

We've decided that Morag shouldn't hear it at all from us. Although, we both realise that there's a growing intimacy between the two of them but we don't feel the need to alarm her. I personally think that Séamus himself should tell Morag about who he is or perhaps if their friendship continues, Morag will find the truth out for herself.

He's told me that he's lived for a 1000 years but has not revealed how he won the battle of ageing with the enemy of us all, time. He's a total mystery in plain human flesh.

The trail of my thoughts is interrupted; Oona is calling me for lunch.

She's sourced local fish from Lochy and has cooked it on coal fire in our workshop fireplace. I'm not very pleased about it thinking that it will stink for days of fish. But as I step in, there is no fish smell there at all. She's done some Icelandic trick but I don't know what.

It's delightful; cooked on coal and nicely seasoned, pleasing to my palate.

She informs me in a tone laced with surprise and suspense that Morag and Séamus are in the Isle of Harris and coming back in a few days.

We both wonder.

Now the trajectory of our conversation takes a different route; our business. We already have a name for it, 'Mackenzie Lodges'. We both know that we need to get the lodges running by summer, so we want to organise ourselves and put the plan into practice as a crash programme to get it done as soon as possible.

We've no idea how long Séamus is going to stay, but he's never mentioned going anywhere else. I personally believe that he's going to be around as he's mentioned his enduring patience previously but Oona thinks that as soon as he finds his bridle, he will want to leave. We just wonder if he'd like to shift between human and kelpie, and come and live alongside us.

It is a beautiful crisp day and we both go out for a long walk. Loch Lochy is on our walking route.

As we walk down the hill, Oona says that we should keep our eyes open when we come out for walks, who knows where the unearthed necklace is in the premises or the estate. I agree with her.

Now we're a party of two in search of this necklace.

***

TIME HAS FLOWN BY very quickly. The house is buzzing with activity. Life after the Christmas has returned to normality. In spite of our failure to find the necklace so far, we're all pleased this morning. There is a reason to celebrate. I think we should take every opportunity to celebrate whenever we can. You never know what's round the corner.

We have the architectural plan of our complex of lodges; contractors have given us the dates when they will land here with their machinery, and the logs have been sourced. Things are looking good.

A Scottish bagpiper is playing outside on the premises.

We've organised a ceremonial breaking of the ground to begin the construction of our log cabins. Oona's brother and parents are there as well. Her brother has given us a loan for the construction. I nominate Séamus as my loyal employee to perform the rituals of breaking the ground.

Afterwards, surprisingly, Séamus asks me if I've mentioned anything to Oona because he thinks she seems a little bit different towards him and has said to him that she knows why he declined the invitation by aunt Jean.

I assure him that there's nothing to be alarmed of. I say that Oona has been teasing him because he was away with

Morag and hadn't mentioned that holiday to us at all. I've satisfied him for the time being but he isn't aware that I can't keep secrets from my wife. It was a huge burden for me; I had to share it.

The first day of our construction work is ending. The site manager is a young man; very enthusiastic, extremely polite and cooperative.

The construction team is leaving now.

These days, Morag isn't around all the time. She's started at college so she comes and goes. She's missed here as she's like a family to us.

Oona is knitting and Séamus is fixing the locking hook of her pearl bracelet that I gave her some time ago.

I didn't intend to eavesdrop but just overhear her asking him, 'So how old are the pearls in Morag's bracelet.'

I need to rescue Séamus. I love my woman but sometimes I don't trust her with her curiosity. If I don't intervene now she will spoil the trust between Séamus and me.

As I step in, Séamus looks at me with questioning eyes but focuses on the fixing job he's doing. I sit beside Oona so that I can change the topic and nudge her to stop if necessary.

Séamus responds, 'They are not ancient...but some hundred years old.'

She seems to be satisfied with his response and says to me to stay with him and be a good company until she fetches us our supper.

Séamus looks at me, 'You've told her...haven't you.'

I admit saying that I couldn't handle this strange truth all by myself...I just had to tell her...Your secret is safe with us.'

We're served our super and Séamus says, 'Oona, now you know...who I am...I guess no one can better handle this truth than the woman from the land of trolls and elves...I have to tell you that I'm bound to this land...You don't need to be scared of me.'

A thick curtain of silence has dropped between us. Oona doesn't know where to look and what to say. She thinks that she's exposed the secret he was trying to hide.

It's an awkward moment. Other than the loud and heavy silence, the sound of knives and forks is hitting our eardrums. Oona touches my leg and I jump embarrassing her and myself too.

She calms me down by the pat of her palm and then unexpectedly asks away, 'Were you always Séamus?'

He throws an accusing look towards me and replies, 'Not really...for a time I was nameless...then someone called me Séamus Chisholm...and I adopted the name since then.'

Oona is full of questions now. She carries on, 'Are you Fraser...the wanderer.'

'Yes...I am.'

Oona hides her face between her hands, 'Oh...my God.'

After a few moments of silence she continues, 'Are these stories of theft and stealing true?'

'Some of them...I had to eat and sleep somewhere warm...so I had to do whatsoever I could...if I took something from any peasant I left them something else.'

I'm full of questions myself and a spectator too watching them unfolding the account of this strange employee of ours.

She poses her next question without any further delay, 'Do you still have anything you stole.'

Séamus says, pointing towards his kilt, 'This McKenzie kilt...I stole it from a chieftain's house but in return I helped the women to spin their wool.'

She further inquiries, 'How old is this kilt?

'Nearly 500 years.'

'How come it's not worn out?

He narrates the same story he's mentioned to me previously, involving a monk and his prayers. She also asks about the antlers he's given her.

He replies, 'I killed that red deer...nearly 400 years ago...The meat lasted for months and these antlers even longer...They are antique.'

Oona is asking, listening and absorbing information faster than she can eat. Her plate is still full so I remind her, 'Words don't satisfy the hunger of the belly.'

Séamus has previously told me about Caitrìona but now I ask him to tell us everything we don't know.

Rowan is barking and we know that he's in the workshop. Oona suggests that we all go there. Séamus immediately leaves for downstairs and I help Oona in tidying up.

Our workshop is dimly lit, Séamus has put more logs in the fire and it's leaping and roaring. Oona has brought a thick blanket for herself and has covered herself sitting next to me. We're sitting again in awkward silence.

Séamus has taken Rowan on his lap, he kisses his beloved dog and he starts his story,

'I've lived for a long time and to be honest I'm tired of living. It's difficult to be a human...but it's a curse to be human and live forever. I'm under this curse. Immortality and humanity should never go together. I've tasted its bitter fruit though; it tastes sweet to start with...I know people will give anything to be immortal; I've met many of them. I've seen and lived too much of life and have no desire to continue so. You'd wonder why I say that...Life is a gift to mortal beings so it is worth enjoying as a gift. I guess, you have no idea that the beings who live forever, envy you humans so much.'

'I know you're thinking if I'm not human then what I am. I'm a spirit with an ability to transform myself...Why is this spirit a human? To keep things simple...I fell in love.'

'I met Caitrìona on her fishing trips, with her brother, to the Loch. They'd come every now and then and I was a constant presence on the banks of Lochy. I caught her attention as she caught mine. She always found me by the bank. I fell in love with everything she was. Our meetings continued. She started to come alone...She wasn't an ordinary woman. She was the daughter of a chieftain. One day she came alone. After fishing we chatted, I took her to the Loch and swam together. The weather suddenly went from bad to worst. Strong winds picked up and gathered clouds, thunderstorm and lightening frightened her. She was scared to go home alone but she didn't want me to accompany her either. It was a death sentence to be seen with another man. She was betrothed to the son of another chieftain. So she wanted to keep our meetings secret. She needed my help.'

'I told her to stay under the tree and wait for my horse to arrive. I told her just to jump on it and it would take her to her house. The job was done. She was home safe.'

'After a few days, she came back. The weather was better. She immediately said to me, "Where is your black strong stallion? He ran like the wind." I was still looking at her and thinking what to say when she said, "I know who you are "

'I'd have thought that she'd be scared to come alone to the Loch and wouldn't see me again but I was wrong. She told me that her grandmother had an encounter with a water spirit and the spirit saved her life. So Caitrìona knew I was a Kelpie.'

'Months passed and we continued seeing each other. I wanted her to be with me, and I was ready to be available when she could come to the banks. But she wanted more than that. I was in love with a mortal and she wanted to have me by her side always...She told me that she had a plan. It was the month of January and we still had to wait for this plan. She didn't say much to me about her plan. She just indicated that she needed to get away for Easter morning. She wanted me to take her to this special place, she wanted to go to.'

'During this period, I frequently transformed myself and went to her nearby settlement. Nobody knew who I was but people were cautious of the arrival of any stranger. Those were the times when you'd be suspicious of anything even guests and members of your family. You never knew who was with you or against you. She told me not to be a bold presence in the village. I took her advice and kept myself away from the village.'

'Easter season arrived, Caitrìona made all the arrangements. She came to see me by the bank with her friend and asked me to wait by her bedroom window that night.'

'I was there as soon as the sun set beyond the mountains. When the house was quiet, Caitrìona jumped down from her window and I was there to help. Dogs barked and horses neighed but Caitrìona was riding a Kelpie. She was safe with me. I was at her service; she rode me and directed me where to go.'

'When we arrived near the pool, she told me what was going to happen. By the pool, early in the morning when the first ray of sun touches the earth, a mermaid comes out of the pool...The legend is that whoever the mermaid favours on Easter morning, gets the gift of eternal life...and she wished to be an immortal.'

'She also told me that there were stories of a woman from her village long time ago who got the gift of immortality...Catriona was very pretty, no one could resist her sweet beauty...Her crystal blue eyes...I could stare at them for thousand years.'

'Well...she opened her satchel and took out a little bundle and unrolled it. She had everything she needed. She changed into beautiful clothes, slipped her creamy white feet into silver sandals studded with jewels and little jingling bells. She was the daughter of a chieftain. Everything she put on was fit for a princess. She told me that her mother had made the dress and sandals for her wedding. She wanted to look like a princess for eternity.'

'She got ready to walk beside the pool. Then she looked at me, took out another bundle, a relatively bigger one and handed it to me saying, ''When I become immortal, I want you to be the first person to see me...so get ready...I'll call you Séamus Chisholm.''

'I put on the kilt that she'd brought for me and the shoes and everything else she had for me. I was ready to walk by her side.'

'We stood beside the pool; there were other people before us wanting to be immortal. Only one would be favoured and the rest of them were going to be disappointed.'

'We waited for a bit. The pool water started to bubble and shimmer as if the stars had fallen in to it. It was a small pool but the roar of water was like a thunder storm and just after that rumble and thunder, a mermaid came out of the water and sat on a stone by the pool.'

'People started to walk in front of her. She smiled at Caitrìona and as her smile lingered and eyes shifted...She blinked...Her eyes fixed on me, with an outlandish smile. Caitrìona had told me that we'd have to wait for everyone to have passed before the mermaid.'

'As soon as everyone had their chance to walk, the mermaid vanished into the small pool of water and everyone started to take their shoes off. I wasn't sure what was happening. I helped Caitrìona to take her feet out of her jingling sandals. She looked at her feet in panic and was disappointed. She threw her shoes away and cried.'

'I didn't know what was happening. She said, "I'm sorry, I wasn't favoured by the mermaid...whoever becomes immortal gets a sign...their toenails shimmer like mermaid's body scales." Unfortunately, Caitrìona's toenails didn't glisten. I was disappointed as well but Caitrìona was really heartbroken.'

'Now we had to hurry, the first sun rays had struck the earth and the morning was marching on. Caitrìona needed to be home as soon as possible.'

'Before she went back through her window, she gave me pendent shaped like a horse head and my own silver chain saying, "These pendants have been carved from a single piece of silver...and the old lady who made them told me that people who would wear them around their necks, it will bind their souls and hearts...put it on now."

'Caitrìona rushed through the window...I put my silver chain around my neck but I couldn't shape shift...Immediately, I realised that my chain was swapped with Caitrìona's...I couldn't wait there. The place was littered with dogs and horses. I left the place immediately...I had to wait for her to come back to me...I walked back to the Loch in my kilt with the name she gave me...I waited for her for few days but she didn't come back and I couldn't go to her house...Her father had many horses. They'd have galloped, got frightened and would have betrayed me.

'One day, I couldn't hear the call of my bridle...I was restless. She came back in the evening without it, I knew she didn't have my bridle. She told me that her stepmother had caught her red handed and taken the chain and the pendent. She had told her mother that it was a spell bound chain and pendent and that the gems could drive her mad...so perhaps the step mother buried the chain with the pendent somewhere. I was so mad and devastated but she promised to find it for me.'

'Sitting beside the Loch, I took my shoes off, when she and her friend came by a few days later. She saw my shimmering toenails and screamed, blaming that I had stolen the mermaid's heart as she bestowed immortality on me. She was jealous beyond measure, nearly at the brink of madness. I wasn't even aware of what had happened to me until I took my socks off. I tried to wash my toenails but the shimmer and pearly hues wouldn't go away. I was stuck in human body but also unaware that immortality has struck me too...so here I am.'

Silence has hit the room and all three of us.

It's deafening now and I dare to punctuate it. I ask, 'So you crashed into something which seems outlandish to us and unpleasant to you. I guess you are not human but you are in a way...and immortality isn't part of the nature...the world at least I know. Tell me, what's more troublesome to you...being a human or being an immortal.'

He sighs, 'I'm not tired of being human...during this bizarre course of my long life, I've met some wonderful individuals of your kind, have lived with them, fought with them, wept with them, fallen in love, have been father to some fatherless kids but I've lost my freedom to come and go from your world into mine...You don't understand and I don't blame you... but being human, all the time, is tiresome. I cry for my waters and I love your land. But the most terrible thing is having no choice.'

I offer him a shot of Lochy. I know he appreciates it. Now I also want to know what he thinks of immortality. I shouldn't rush him and must wait for him. He swirls his Lochy, drinks, and smiles, and asks for more. He seems to be in deep thoughts far away, may be trying to span the 1000 years he has lived for.

Eventually, he speaks again after hearing swooshing and swishing sounds of fabric indicating our shifting and changing positions on the sofa.

'Well, I don't mind biological immortality. I enjoy youthfulness...I don't worry about getting old but I fear the day when I'm stuck in this human body and this bestowed immortality wears off or is taken away from me. I don't know the feeling of what it means to be old in body but I can tell, it is the worst thing to happen to humanity. Getting old is the painful flaw in the planning of your kind...I've witnessed some terrible incidents of human suffering just because they get old. A perfectly capable individual can be reduced to such a pitiable state in old age...But the immortality of thoughts, feelings and experiences is something incredibly painful. I've lost countless dear friends and lovers. It hurts to see them grow old and decrepit. With my biological immortality, the burden of my loss is immortal too...Any wrongdoing, any careless move, any unthoughtful words and actions haunt me. My suffering is greater than those who passed away in suffering...The world is so unkind, being human is an enough punishment but being an immortal on top of being human is painful.'

'The ONE who is immortal forever knows it well and is wise. Why do you think that the tree of life in the Garden of Eden was guarded by the Cherubim and a Flaming Sword?'

He has been revealing his knowledge about all sorts of things all along since he's been with us, but I'm astonished that he knows about religion as well. So you know I can't not question him and his response is,

'Well when you have to live in the world, you need to know and learn about it. So I've been to various learning places, studied numerous subjects depending on the age I lived in. To name a few, I've studied art, dance, science, medicine and religions of course…remember I had to reinvent myself quite often.'

To be honest, I cannot explain what I feel after hearing this account from one freakish being sitting with us. Oona says to him,

'I can't not be a bit fearful of what life is…especially as there might be so many aspects of it which we aren't even aware of.'

He immediately responds, 'Being a friend, employee or whatever, take my advice: live your life; it is meant to be lived…contemplating on what actually it is…no one has or is going to have an answer in your life time…so don't lose sleep over it.'

I know in my heart of hearts that Oona and myself, leaving business out of this equation, have grown to love him. It was a hell of a confusion for me knowing he wasn't what we thought he was. He is a shape shifter. It has freaked us out but we still care for him and it isn't an exaggeration that we actually truly love him and feel as if he's part of our family even if he isn't one of our own kind in reality. I wonder how he feels about us.

He says, 'Companionship is a strange feeling; it doesn't care about the kind...You can love a wild raven or a fox in the wild and they will be by your side...I know it's outlandish to you but I've lived with ravens and squirrels...As long as you are not nasty to them and are ready to co-exist with mutual respect and care...the kind of a being does not matter.'

Now Oona feels sorry for him and comments, 'aww...I'm sad that you've lost so much in all those years...but it just sounds like a charming fairy-tale.'

He becomes annoyed, 'For you humans every unusual and inexplicable event is a fairy tale...I have told you a true tale of my life...Open your eyes...Look around...Life is more than just what your senses can tell you...Oona, you should know better than that!'

Oona is a little flabbergasted as she didn't mean what he thinks she meant. She apologises, 'I don't mean that it's a lie...it's just that we've been told all these stories or...events...as fairy tales.'

Séamus leaves the room with Rowan in his arms. Oona is holding me tight. We both are silent; thinking that perhaps he's becoming distant and temperamental.

I put some more logs in the fire. I don't think we can sleep tonight after this revelation. We both feel a bit edgy but not particularly scared. Oona is sad that unintentionally she's upset Séamus. She wishes he'd tell us about Caitrìona. What happened to her and to him later as well.

I tell Oona what I guess comes after that is the period of 'Fraser the wanderer' which he's talked about earlier.

In all this time, Oona surprises me the most. In spite of the stories of huldufólk deeply trenched in her culture, she can't believe that he's a kelpie, and that she needs to see some evidence.

This whole saga of Séamus has affected our thinking. I'm doubting what I've been taught, and my world view and frame of thinking seems shaky; Oona, though, believes in trolls and elves, yet, asks for some evidence of his claim.

***

LIFE GOES ON IN SPITE of these bizarre revelations and weird encounters. Oona and myself have been home alone with Rowan; apprehensive and suspicious, grateful and what not.

Séamus has just come back today from somewhere after being absent for nearly a week. I don't ask him anything. Today, he's again the same relaxed and patient Séamus. I'm sure, he was in Harris but he's back and that's enough for me. He's spent the whole day in the workshop and has accomplished a load of work.

Oona has helped him with the post office run and the packing of the parcels. She's truly satisfied with today's work because we weren't sure whether he was coming back to us or not.

Oona has just walked in announcing that Séamus wants us to go to Harris over the weekend. In her opinion, he wants to prove that his story isn't a fairy-tale. He wants to show us something. He can't shape shift but he wants to show us that he's been around for a long time.

Oona is incredibly excited but I'm apprehensive. Aunt Jean's words echo in my head, 'They're vicious creatures.' Oona disagrees saying that he's been a 'wanderer' as well. There is some goodness in him. He's been kind to the peasants and has been amazing to us. Although, she is right, however, I still can't shake the thought that he can turn malicious towards us.

In all this hustle and bustle, I haven't forgotten about his necklace. I've been looking for it. I've been moving things around in the basement but with no success so far.

A part of me wants to find it immediately and a bit of me wishes that it's never found. I sound selfish but he's the goose that lays the golden eggs. Who would want to lose him?

In spite of all these selfish thoughts, you have to believe that he's become family to me with all his freakish existence.

**

I HAVE LIVED NEARLY all my life in Scotland but I have never had the chance to visit the Hebrides. It's a cloudless day. I can see from the window: the beautiful green stretches of land in the middle of a huge expanse of blue and green waters. The land is studded with clusters of buildings. In spite of its beauty, the land feels very desolate.

I'm still getting used to my seat and suddenly, I hear the announcement that we're going to land soon; the shortest plane journey I've ever taken.

Our hired car is waiting for us and so is Séamus with fresh fish from the harbour.

We arrive at a self-catering cottage and guess what the cottage is called: 'kelpie cottage'. Séamus informs us that it's a traditional stone Hebridean cottage. I'm very impressed, as it has been thoughtfully and tastefully modernised. It's cosy and snug.

Oona has already gone out for a walk with Rowan, running ahead of her. Séamus and I are the chefs.

He tells me that a long time ago, he used to live in this cottage, which was incredibly basic then. He has no idea who named this cottage 'kelpie cottage'. He further informs me that he had to move to reinvent himself so he settled in Stornoway for some time.

I tease him saying 'island hopper' and he just smiles as if saying that you have no idea what it means to be a hopper. I guess he needed to have a symbiotic relationship with these islands. Hopping was his strategy for survival.

Although, eventually I've come to terms with the fact that he's not one of us but to tell you the truth my mind is compartmentalised over the reality of his existence. I wonder if I'm passing through a period of cognitive dissonance.

At times, it feels as if I'm dreaming.

Over the meal, in response to our questions, Séamus has told us that Catrioana sadly killed herself. He was no more bound to her. There was no reason to stick around and his bridle had stopped calling so he left for the Isle of Harris.

He's mentioned again that he's eternally bound to Loch Lochy and its surrounding land and our estate is part of that land. I'm relieved that he feels that he has a strong connection to my land but I'm also apprehensive to hear of his bond with humans via the necklace. I know that the last woman who wore that necklace is my aunt Jean. Does he still feel that he's bound to her? I have no idea. I also wonder what's going to happen to Morag. They're incredibly attracted to each other.

We're out of the cottage now. After a short drive, we're walking beside Séamus, not knowing where he wants to take us. The car is parked at the base of this hill. It's not very steep but walking up the hill is still hard. On the other side of the hill, as we begin to descend, we can see the vast ocean stretched out everywhere as far as your human eye permits you to see.

He points towards an uninhabited island saying, 'I once decided to go and live there...when I had to reinvent myself and restart.'

Now he's bent on his knees; removing little stones, all the scattered grass and earth, and then with a rustic key he opens the door. I could have never imagined that there was a door, hidden in plain sight.

He invites us in saying, 'It was my den for a long time, my hiding place.'

To tell you the truth, I don't want to go in. Oona looks apprehensive but she is not sweating like me. I need to man up. I put a brave face on and say to Oona, 'Are you ok to go in?' thinking I'll hide behind her fear. But astonishingly she says that she is fine.

After a bit of contemplation, I eventually decline to go in saying one of us needs to stay out in case something goes wrong. Oona agrees with me and starts to descend following Séamus who has already started to go down.

I'm absurdly happy to be in the open air but also aware of missing out on what he has down there in his den. I lie down on the grass; there's no human in sight except for me but there are many birds coming and going to the sea for their food. I wonder what kind of existence is this when the plan is nothing else but searching for food all day long.

I just snooze a bit and then the forceful opening of the mysterious little door wakes me up. A rustic jute bag is being pushed out. I try to help; Séamus passes me another rustic bag full of something. Bags are out followed by Séamus and then Oona.

She tells me that under this hill, there are many caverns and it is filled with all sorts of treasure almost of 1000 years old.

As Séamus is locking the window-like tiny door, Oona whispers to me, 'You have to believe me; he has lived for a 1000 years. He's shown me stuff down there that you can't imagine even existed...He's really an old soul.'

She unlocks her hand. On her stretched out palm, there are two primitive firestones and some huge pearls as well perched on her palm.

We walk down the hill after Séamus has made sure that his hiding place is concealed and well camouflaged.

He gives me something from his pocket, rolled in strips of old rag, saying, 'It will answer another question of yours which I've answered but vaguely.'

I immediately sit down on driving seat and then I start to unwrap it. I've removed many strips but it is like unpeeling an onion; they keep coming. Eventually, something shiny and metallic comes out with a worn out wooden handle.

No one needs to tell me. I recognise it. It's a huge ancient Scottish dirk.

He tells me that he once got into fight with a man over stealing birds eggs on this very hill and the man attacked him, pointing towards the scar on his face. He snatched it from the man and to my horror, he attacked him back and left him badly injured. He tells me that the injured guy would have not survived.

He indicates, touching his face, that it was the last wound he endured before the monk blessed him.

I'm speechless holding this weapon of murder in my hand as he continues, 'Keep this...It will remind you of my 'bird's egg scar' and, more importantly, remember it inflicts a wound: painful as anything but somehow the wound doesn't bleed.'

His revelations defy the laws of nature, which operate in my world: but so does he, existing side by side us, shocking us every now and then.

***

I TELL YOU EVERYTHING has been superfast, especially, time has flown on the wings of highland winds which have been our constant companions this year. It is already the month of July and it doesn't feel long since we celebrated Christmas.

I'm sitting in god's seat wondering how time cheats us so easily but at the same time, I'm filled with an absurd happiness at the smell of coffee and the sight of my humble golden toast and honey. These simple things seems celestial to me.

Life with all its mystery has been wonderful to us, although Mackenzie Lodges are delayed a little. Construction is complete but the indoor work is still not there yet.

Oona has been in charge of the gardens around the Mackenzie Lodges. One can see Séamus has definitely influenced her decisions. The gardens are just a huge swath of Scottish heather. They've sourced all varieties of heather from the far and near. Séamus keeps saying that these little shrubs bring good luck; and she listens to him and puts into practice what he suggests. I'm not complaining, just stating my observation. The gardens are marvellous as if a piece of land stolen from paradise.

At the main entrance, the 'Mackenzie Lodges' sign is set and even though it is not open for business yet, it is lit up every night. Oona wanted a sculpture of red deer; Séamus has carved two and they're standing inside the main entrance under canopies to protect them from the elements. Oona has mentioned to me a while ago that Séamus wants to add something else to the garden as well but he's not revealed what it will be.

'Beloved Wood' is still busy bringing us a good income.

These days Séamus works during the day in the cabins and at night in our workshop. For the lodges, Séamus has taken care of the kitchen furniture, and the rest of the task force is working on the floor and the bedroom furniture for 10 lodges.

Now, I'm standing in the first finished Lodge and I can't tell you how proud I feel. I'm thrilled to see everywhere I lay my eyes; blessing these gorgeous lodges, and wishing they will always bring comfort and joy to the dwellers. Everything looks fantastic and sometime I still can't believe that the 'Mackenzie Lodges' are nearly finished and belong to us.

Last year has changed me a lot. I know some journeys don't end as planned. I also have grasped the fact that if things are happening, try to believe them even if you don't have a shred of faith left in you.

This tiny, nearly exhausted, shred of faith can do wonders.

***

OONA TELLS ME THAT last night when she was in the workshop working with Séamus, he saddened her.

He said, 'I've come to learn that I should not be living among people...no matter how much I love them or they love me...When you've lived so long, then you know that everyone who has ever loved you is going to die...There's no belonging for me...this world where I'm trapped, is only a happy place when you've people who love you and you love them in return...'

He has told her that he's beginning to feel a part of our little family, and mentioned that is it important to find his bridle but it feels more important to belong and live with people like us.

He sometimes yearn for his waters but he knows once he goes there he'd want to come back to us but we'd not be there forever. So he'd have to start all over and he's tired of starting everything over and over again.

It's made me sad too but I'm pleased that he feels belonging to this family. In spite of all the weird things about him, I sometime feel I've got the younger brother that I never had. I must confess, I deeply care for him. He has won our hearts.

Oona has gone to the cabins, and I'm going to search for his necklace.

It's a beautiful summer morning; a hell of a memory for me to carry through the dark days that winter will bring.

All the windows and doors are wide opened; light has filled every nook and corner of this house. As far as you can see, it's all about freshness of green and intense brightness; nearby hot pinks and sunshine yellows grow in the garden and have transformed the place. This is a magical makeover of my land. It is going to be the best summer of my life.

I can't stand here and marvel at my assets. I'm going in the basement. I have to remove all the boxes; examine the floor, and look for this specific brick again.

As I make my way to the basement, I have a strange feeling. I can sense in my bones that something is going to happen which is going to either excite me or sadden me. I don't know how I can tell this but it feels as if it's predetermined.

I have already noticed a number of weird looking bricks, but none of them can be moved. They're fixed to the ground. Suddenly, I trip over something and I'm on the floor. My forehead is sore but not bleeding. I immediately get back and see that one brick is more worn out than the surrounding ones and is a little bit more dipped in the ground. With a considerable effort, I manage to remove it and I can't believe my eyes. There's a little compartment under the brick stuffed with things.

I take out everything. At the bottom, there's a wooden box. I take it out too and open it expectantly. It's filled with jewellery. I can see a shiny chain with a pendent badly entangled with other chains. There are loads of them. I'm carefully trying to disentangle it but with a jerky pull, to my horror, the pendent falls on the ground and the chain is broken.

I'm panicking...I know when his bridle is unearthed it calls him...I immediately shove everything back in the little cell under the brick.

I'm incredibly sad that I've broken the chain, and the broken bridle is good for nothing, he has told me. I remove the brick again, trying to loosen the knots that have tied the multiple chains without taking them out of the cell, wishing that I could get rid of his bridle from the bondage of other chains. In this struggle, now it is broken at two other places.

I sit there and wonder what to do.

I take out the pendant; it's very light in spite of its considerable size. It binds soul, he says, but all he wants is his bridle back that is now broken sitting in the cell under the brick. I put the pendent back with the shiny bridle and leave.

I need to think through what to do. It's good news but I can't tell Séamus until it is fixed. I've come to offer help in the Lodges thinking it will take my mind off the broken bridle.

As I walk down the hill towards the cabins, I suddenly recall that I have a schoolmate from the area who is a silversmith. I turn back immediately, get the chain from the brick cell, put it in a tiny plastic bag and then hide it in the soil of an abandoned flower pot from our kitchen garden and drive down to see him.

I'm in his shop. I'm not a jeweller but I can tell you that in the display area no chain is as lustrous as his bridle. It feels magical just like its owner. I'm waiting for my turn, holding the flowerpot tightly to my chest and getting a few quizzical looks from the fellow customers.

Josh, my silversmith friend, takes me in and I show him the chain in the secrecy of his workshop. I'm not surprised that he's dazzled by the lustrous silver chain I hand him. He says, 'It's not a big deal to put it together...It can be done quickly but not today.'

Obviously, it's too precious to be left anywhere; I have to guard it with my life. So I take it back safely hidden under the soil in this flowerpot.

As I enter the house, the three of them are sitting around the table. I don't pay attention to them, but run back to the basement and hide the flowerpot in the cell.

As I join them, I'm told that in the 'Mackenzie Lodges' all the indoor work is finished now. The delivery for bedding, towels and other things required for the rooms and bathrooms is arriving today. Morag's come to help with getting the lodges ready.

Oona particularly informs me that both the modern and the ancient Mackenzie tartan is featured in every room. She puts a huge joyful stress on 'Mackenzie'. Furthermore, the walls are decked with beautiful artwork. One of the paintings from Séamus's den is hanging at the main entrance.

They tell me of the success in the lodges, and I've found the necklace, although it is still hidden under the ground. Good progress at each end. No one needs to know about the necklace yet.

***

I'VE JUST WOKEN UP; feeling dispirited, over breaking the chain accidentally, but at the same time hope in Josh's skill has given me a positive outlook as I recall his words.

Coming down the stairs, I hear that the kitchen is buzzing with morning humdrum activities and smells. Oona's humming something endlessly as she whisks the eggs. I put my arms around her neck kissing her head. I know she's filled with joy. Her eyes have a twinkle when she gives me that special look. I see peace, serenity, and a sense of satisfaction on my woman's face and I love her dearly. She's my rock and anchor. Without her, I am lost.

Don't get me wrong. I'm not a total miserable soul. I'm happy too that the Mackenzie Lodges are standing proud and tall. It feels as if they've just grown out of the ground. To be honest, I have lost the sense of time. It feels as if it was just a week ago when we were discussing our project and now the product of our dreams has come into being.

Many things have changed. The four of us seem to be a family and the bond between us has grown strong in spite of all the weird stuff happening. I feel there is a great camaraderie and a deep sense of care and love amongst us. Knowing an immortal being resides with us, means that I can't forget how ephemeral life is. I truly wish that this bond will last as long as we live.

Turning towards me, Oona reminds me sternly that I have to work with her today as we're going to make the Lodges ready before the end of the day. She tells me that Morag and Séamus have already gone and mentions how inseparable they are. I wonder if he's said anything to Morag, but I feel this shouldn't be my headache today at all. I've something else on my mind.

I have my breakfast and I'm ready to start my day, but I'm waiting for Oona to leave the house so that I can get the flowerpot from the basement. However, she's determined to take me with her to the lodges. I've argued a little but I know I have no choice.

As I wander around the lodges, I can't tell you the sensation I feel; it almost gives me goose bumps.

Morag and I are putting a special painting in the lobby. This painting also came from Séamus's den. It's of a magnificent highland cattle. Morag is unaware of the origin of this piece but she admires it. It's too huge and heavy for Morag to lift it; Séamus steps in to help.

I look around and realise that Morag has slipped out, I ask him, 'What's the history behind this?' He replies that he bought it from an artist, selling his paintings on the street, just because the artist was desperate to sell it.'

He immediately asks if there's any progress on the necklace. I wonder if he heard his bridle's call when I took it out of the ground. I'm not ready to tell him yet, especially the bad news. I hope to get it fixed. I calm myself quickly, reassuring him that I have some inkling so it will not be too long.

After a moment, I leave the cabins telling Séamus that I'll be back soon. I'm driving down the hill faster, nervous and full of guilt.

I regain assurance from Josh. He asks me to leave it with him and collect it latter. He can sense my hesitance. I can't afford to do this so I insist that I have time to spare and perfectly happy to stay and chat with him too. He curiously asks me, 'Why this strange pot?' and I simply say, 'It's a family heirloom and just for protection.

He gives me quizzical looks muttering, 'A flower pot for protection.'

The dazzling silver chain is on the table. He's surprised by the radiance of the chain; he asks again if it is silver.

I'm sitting nearby and ready to watch the restoration of his bridle. Josh has put some special little tools beside him. He's put glass over his own glasses. He changes it two three times, feeling frustrated. He also has a little jar full of tweezer like tools close to him; he's picking one tweezer after the other but in vain.

He sighs telling me that the chain links feel so slippery. His tools are slithering over the chain links. He rubs the chain with a cloth again.

I don't know what to feel; surprised or annoyed. His tools seem to have no grip on these chain links. He asks me again if the metal is silver. I reassure him. He asks to test the metal. He has noticed my hesitancy. I don't know what to do. In desperation to get it fixed, I think I can sacrifice one chain link.

Josh immerses one chain link into a liquid from a tiny cute bottle. The chain link has changed it silveriness into creamy white suggesting that it is silver for sure. But he still looks baffled by the brightness of the chain and suspects that its shine has been enhanced somehow.

I ask him if there's another way to get it restored.

He understands that it belongs to my family and is essential that I get it restored but he can't do anything about it. He suggests checking with other silversmiths but also suspects that they wouldn't do anything that he hasn't already done. Above all, I don't want to take this chain to every Tom, Dick and Harry. It needs to be done in secrecy.

Speculating and taking the special glass off from his eye he says, 'I wish I could save it from the furnace...I can't put the links together...but I can melt it to change into something else.'

His suggestion sends chill through my spine because I'm not sure about any other prospect of this chain. I need some time to think. I leave, with my flowerpot, frustrated and guilty.

As I sit in the car, I try to recall everything Séamus has said about this chain. It has to be around his neck touching his body. Suddenly an idea strikes. I think if I can get it changed into a medallion and then put into a chain it will be around his neck touching his body. Perhaps that will do the job.

I feel stupid and annoyed at myself. I can't understand how I managed to break the chain in spite of all the care I had taken.

The guilt of my mistake has paralysed me and I can't tell, not even to Oona. I just have to deal with it myself.

***

THE SMELL OF A SUMMER DAY is still lingering in the air. We have organised a huge barbecue in our back garden. It's been hard to persuade Séamus to stay for barbecue. He didn't want to be around aunt Jean. He's promised to be around tomorrow. We've never hosted such a huge group of guests before just like many things, which we had never come across, experienced or done before.

It feels strange but I believe when unusual and crazy things start to happen, you are in preparation for some epic eventuality.

We've just double-checked all the engagements for tomorrow's opening ceremony. Tomorrow Mackenzie Lodges will be officially opened for business. We're looking forward to welcome many local dignitaries and actually most of the neighbours nearby.

Our families have come from Devon and Iceland.

Oona's parents are impressed with the lay out, craftsman ship, the elegant taste, and the calm and cosy feel in and around the cabins. I feel incredibly proud to be a Mackenzie. I want to tell uncle Harrison that we Mackenzies can do more than just coffee making, as he often teases us. Aunt Jean hasn't seen anything yet. She has to wait until tomorrow.

A beautiful cool August evening has claimed the vast land. We feel a little chill in the air. Oona and I are just having a last walk around the complex before calling it a night. It feels so satisfying to see these lodges in their beauty standing graceful, matching up with the natural beauty of the surroundings. Pride fills me like a balloon and this pride needs some venting out...I begin to whistle.

Oona is clinging to me. I know she needs her shawl. I go and get it for her before we go to the back garden of the lodges. As we walk, the incredible colours of various varieties of heather and different arrangement of these superb shrubs scattered among Rowan trees is truly charming. I've never paid attention to this lowly shrub before but it has transformed our garden's outlook.

We just turn round the corner and we can't believe our eyes. Our jaws drop, eyes forget to blink and perhaps hearts skipped a beat too. I sit on the nearby bench, totally astonished...Guess what we see...There are 10 medium sized wooden horses gracing the garden. There are no words to describe our utter amazement.

Oona breaks the silence; I can hear her sniffling. She's overwhelmed, tremendously. I gather her into my arms. In her sniffles and sobs she says, 'This is what his last surprise for this complex is...in all this hustle and bustle I'd forgotten about it...Oh my God...How are we ever going to repay him for his hard work...I wish he'd stay here with us like our family.'

I smile saying, 'I feel he's my younger brother...the brother I never had.'

In spite of all her care and love for Séamus, Oona has never mentioned him as family before. I am pleased she feels that way too.

***

WE ARE BEYOND TIRED. Before we sleep, I have something to show Oona. It might warm her heart. I take out the little box I got from Josh. She's a little annoyed that I haven't told her before. I explain the accident with the chain and everything that I've done. I show her Séamus's original pendent cleaned and polished: horse head with two red gems, the soul binder.

She says that she had seen something like that before. I immediately ask her where she saw this. She tells me that last year she found it in the basement before she went to Iceland but then put it back.

Now it's my turn to be annoyed that she didn't mention it to me at all. But she didn't know the importance of it then. I guess, it was that time when Séamus heard his bridle calling and came to our door just when Oona left for Iceland.

I show her a chain with a perfect round medallion in it. This smooth silver disc is not ordinary at all. It has inscription on it running around the edges. It reads 'You are a Mackenzie.' A big smile spreads on Oona's face as she takes it from my hand. She says that it's a magnificently beautiful thought, and belonging seems incredibly important to him.

She also has noticed that its brilliance is no match to the chain. I tell her the whole story from the broken chain to this Mackenzie medallion. I share my apprehension about the broken chain. We both agree that he needs to have his silver next to his body and his silver he will get. Oona thinks we should give his original pendent to Morag. He'd like her wearing it. I'm a little uncertain about it but I shouldn't be doubtful endlessly about each and everything.

I can't sleep tonight. My body is under the influence of excitement and nervousness for tomorrow. Before I sleep, I feel the need to look at our transformed estate from god's seat. I don't have a fuller view from this window now, but I can see the 'Mackenzie Lodges' sign above the entrance, lit up. It's enough to give me tickles tonight.

I lift my eyes up to the sky. It's a moonless night; millions of stars are on display. Suddenly, there's a curtain of moving lights descending from nowhere. Night cannot be more charming. I immediately run back to get Oona. She needs to witness this magic filled night. Tonight, we have witnessed our first aurora borealis since we've been married.

It's been an exciting, hell of a freakish and productive year. Everything still feels so surreal to me. Immersed in our thoughts, we stand speechless for a while. Then Oona speaks gently, 'So much goodness and too much success is frightening me.'

Oona's expression has sent a chill through my spine as we move back to our bedroom.

***

THE DAY HAS ARRIVED; a day of celebrating our achievement and the joy of belonging. I'm up since the crack of the dawn. A strange, unknown and unnamed feeling hangs in the chasm of my chest, which I can't fathom.

I'm clinging to Oona like a barnacle to a ship's hull. Strangely, I don't want to get up as if hesitant to face this day.

Oona whispers in my ear, 'Being nervous is normal...This is what we wanted and today we have it...a complex of lodges, family and friends to join us and Séamus...to become one of us...a Mackenzie.'

Guests have already started to arrive.

The premises near the entrance is filling quickly with people. Aunt Jean is mingling and talking to the crowd. She's always been our social butterfly. I'm so pleased that she's around. Her presence always takes away the feeling that I have, of being a lonely Mackenzie living on the top of this hill.

It's a little breezy, the sky is clear but not as it's been for some weeks; clouds are creeping up from the edge of the blue sky. I hope that the opening ceremony will be over by the time it is overcast.

Oona is by my side as we walk towards the crowd now. The sound of a Scottish piper has filled the air around us. My nieces accompany Morag. They're delivering the brochures for the 'Mackenzie Lodges.' Unfortunately, Séamus is nowhere to be seen. He promised that he'd be around. None of us has seen him since morning but Morag spoke to him earlier when he was going towards Lochy.

People from our neighbourhood are excited and are impressed with what they see in the brochure. Aunt Jean is talking to some old acquaintance and is amused as she reads the brochure, 'Enjoy nature, fish in the nearby Loch Lochy and spot kelpies if you can.' The woman replies,

'You never know...some tourists might just come for this.'

I agree with her, 'You never know, the unexpected has happened in this part of the world.'

Aunt Jean has cut the ribbon, and along with Oona, is now leading the guests to the one lodge opened for our visitors today. Aunt Jean is thrilled with what she sees; she can't contain her joy. She hugs me and a stream of tears has dampened her face. She wipes her eyes and tells me 'Look who's coming.'

I turn round and it is he: the awaited one. We exchange a hug, and a handshake with aunt Jean but she hugs him. Her one hand is on his shoulder and the other around my waist as she says, 'I told you... Séamus is the best employee...I was so right, look at what you've achieved with him...now don't let him go.'

She winks as she ruffles his long hair and then turns towards Rowan, lifting him up she walks away from us.

He sees a complaint in my eye, and says, 'I was around as I said...in the background...behind the garden.'

I have a little sympathy for him, as his woman is here, who never returned his necklace...She doesn't even recognise him and it's painful for him.

Oona and I have just finished a presentation on 'Mackenzie Lodges' and our website has gone live now.

People are moving in and out. We haven't seen so many people on our estate before this for a very long time. The fate of this land has changed incredibly fast. Luxurious tea has been served; whisky is in full demand as well. I wish for a glass of Lochy. There isn't enough for my guests. It's only for us tonight; the last bottle to be shared.

We all stand to say thanks to the people for coming, giving them a goodwill gesture: a pack of five notecards that Oona has designed and painted, depicting the scenes from Loch Lochy and 'Mackenzie Lodges.'

People are walking away from the lodges, and wind is picking up as we finish.

We are open for business tomorrow.

***

EVERYONE IS IN THE LOUNGE except for Morag; she's packing small gifts for the family from 'Beloved Wood.' Oona wants to share our humble fortune.

Aunt Jean has found Séamus and is talking to him in spite of his hesitancy and avoidance. I know, she feels guilty that she was unkind to Séamus senior by keeping his chain. I guess, she's trying to compensate by being kind to his grandson, as she calls him.

Oona and I exchange glances as we overhear what aunt has just said to him, 'When you find that pendent...I suggest you give it to lovely Morag...I notice...she's crazy about you.'

Aunt has asked for whisky now. We have had endless tea and coffee. She likes her whisky, the real McCoy. That's reserved for us to night. It is only aunt Jean, Séamus and I who have the fine palate to enjoy Lochy. This is the last bottle of Lochy, reserved to be shared and enjoyed with the one who knew, created and tasted Lochy long before us.

Suddenly, Séamus is looking for Morag, a sort of urgency in his manner. I point him downstairs, and with a bit of delay I follow him.

I'm standing in the door, horrified.

He approaches Morag, kisses her hard and asks, 'What have you done with my chain?'

Poor Morag is puzzled saying 'I have no chain of yours.'

He pulls his pendent from her neck forcefully, leaving Morag tearful and humiliated. Oona intervenes, pulling Morag towards her and says, 'I've given her this pendant.'

He's going crazy turning towards Oona, 'Where did you get this from?...Where's my bridle?'

He's speaking incredibly loud. We don't recognise his sound. We haven't seen him like this. All the traces of kindliness, trust and camaraderie are gone from his face and voice. I close the door behind me saying, 'I have your chain.'

As he gets out of Oona's way, she takes Morag out.

I take my family Bible from the table and pull out a little box from the central hole.

He takes it from my hand and keeps saying, 'My bridle isn't here...I can't hear it calling me...Where is it...What did you do.'

I tell him, 'This is your silver; put it around your neck.'

'This is not mine,' he screams.

I take it from him and put it around his neck. No shape shifting happens even though medallion is around his neck. His eyes are blood red; he looks so aggressive, pacing around the room.

I tell him, 'When I found the chain, it got broken... It was not of any use to you...I got it melted into this disc.'

He shouts back, 'A Chisholm silversmith could have mended it...The pendent bound to it was forged in a Chisholm smithy.'

He pulls the chain and it breaks. He is holding the silver disc in his hand reading the inscription on it. He actually cries,

'You slaved me here...took advantage of me...lied to me...betrayed me...I am not a Mackenzie...I am a fucking cursed horse...I want to go back to my waters...I can never be a Mackenzie...You are the second one to deceive me.'

I just realise aunt Jean is standing beside the door listening to our conversation.

She walks towards us, 'You have his fiery temperament as well.'

I immediately say, 'It is him, aunt...There was no Séamus senior...He lied to me...It's him'

He turns to aunt Jean, 'If only you have returned my chain then....' He has not finished his sentence and aunt Jean faints. She is on the floor.

Oona rushes down in response to my call and shifts aunt on the floor rug.

I pick up the silver medallion, which he has thrown on the floor, 'You told me that broken chain was good for nothing.'

'It was only broken...not useless...Why did you not tell me.'

He comes forward, takes the medallion from my hand, and throws the pendent which he snatched from Morag, in the fire, 'I don't need to be bound to any human...this is what you do...betray. No wonder I'm more human than most humans.'

He has picked up the dirk he gave me from his den and takes his Tartan saying, 'I am not a Mackenzie' and is about to walk out.

I rush to the door trying to block his way so that we can talk. He is furious...and I'm unhappy too. He cries and warns me to move. I don't move and he throws his dirk stabbing my leg.

I'm on the floor in agony. My leg is on fire but I can't pull it out.

Oona rushes towards me to get it out. There's no blood as he said but a considerable gash and indescribable pain. Oona quickly ties it up, and I walk out.

It's a heavy thunderstorm outside. I can still see him running down the hill with Rowan on his shoulders.

I run after him as fast as I can...calling him back. I know I can't catch him...I, the humble human, and no match for a shape shifter but I still keep following him in anticipation that I might get a bit closer to him or he might turn around. He keeps running and I don't give up either. Hope is the last thing to die and I cling to it.

Now Oona has followed me. I can hear her calling both of us...I suddenly slip and fall over. Oona is trying to lead me back. I can't hear what she says.

His words are very loud in my head.

'I'm not a Mackenzie….I'm a fucking cursed horse…I can never be a Mackenzie…you are the second one to deceive me…I'm not a Mackenzie…I'm not a Mackenzie…I'm not a Mackenzie…'

I don't remember what happened after that.

Oona has, gently, woken me up. Aunt Jean and Morag are standing beside the bed. I search their vacant eyes and look around the room. I don't see him.

My eyes well up again. He came on a sunny day and left us in a storm. The tempest within me is pouring through my eyes, and is going to last longer than the rainstorm outside.

Eventually, the storm has calmed outside…the rain is gone and so is he…gone…gone.

***

«Epilogue»

Many years have passed. I'm sitting at my favourite place, god's seat, watching the Mackenzie Lodges. The Scottish weather has not affected the flow of guests.

I can't forget the day the lodges were opened. I lost him that very day. Aunt Jean died after a few months. The shock of knowing who he was never left her.

Morag stayed for six months helping us with running the lodges. She's gone to live in Iceland now. She's married to Oona's brother. She runs her own restaurant and has three beautiful kids of her own. We often visit them.

Oona, my rock, has given me two beautiful children. My house is fuller and my heart is bursting with love for them. I never knew one can love this much. I wish they know how much I adore them.

Years later, I still have his pendent; the soul binder. He threw it in the fire before leaving. Recently, on multiple occasions, guests have reported a beautiful horse with a shiny bridle and a studded saddle galloping around our estate. I have never seen that horse, nor has Oona.

I turn 60 today. I am not a lonely Mackenzie any more. I have a son and a daughter. I call my son Alexius, an Icelandic name, after Oona's dad. No more Séamus or Hamish from now on.

I'm going to share the last bottle of Loch Lochy tonight with my son, and a part of me wishes that he, Séamus, would come back tonight to share the last bottle.

Now, I can see that my son is coming home. He is a great athlete and loves running. He wants to become an astronomer. He is saving money to buy his first telescope. We both love stargazing. After all these years, the night sky with its celestial bodies still fascinates me.

He's late for dinner tonight; his younger sister, Jean, is annoyed. I will go to meet him half way through.

He tells me that he has seen a strange horse with shiny hooves outside the estate, and it took him a while to pick seaweeds from his wavy mane. His description has given me goose bumps.

I look behind as we walk back to our house, and amusingly enough, I pray for protection from outlandish and freakish beings.

I pour whisky for Oona, Séamus and myself. Jean is too young for this drink. My son loves Lochy and has just surprised me, 'Dad, it would be fun to run a distillery at some point...so it might not be the last bottle of Lochy.'

I am startled with the idea of distillery and that a friend of his, from Harris, is willing to be a partner in the business. Life is never boring but I don't dare to ask his friend's name.

His soul binder pendent was out today; I actually wore it and I wonder.

A horse with shiny hooves has appeared...I wonder.

《　》

A note from the Author

Thank you very much for reading 'Year of the Horse'. I hope you enjoyed this book. Please take a moment to leave a review at amazon online bookstore.

https://www.amazon.co.uk/Year-Horse-Shejee-Hunter-ebook/dp/B07X3DGXMV/ref=sr_1_1?keywords=year+of+the+horse&qid=1568462031&s=books&sr=1-1

Your reviews help other readers to discover the books they might like. You don't have to leave a detailed review. Just say how you enjoyed the book.

Printed in Poland
by Amazon Fulfillment
Poland Sp. z o.o., Wrocław

49690055R00113